Christmas Secrets

by

Pam Binder

Christmas in the Castle

Christmas Secrets

Cover Art by *Lisa Dawn MacDonald*

The Wild Rose Press, Inc.
PO Box 708
Adams Basin, NY 14410-0708
Visit us at www.thewildrosepress.com

Publishing History
First Edition, 2024
Trade Paperback ISBN 978-1-5092-5876-5
Digital ISBN 978-1-5092-5877-2

Christmas in the Castle
Published in the United States of America

Dedication

To my grandmother, Irene,
who loved to tell romantic bedtime stories.
I have never forgotten them.

Prologue

December 1814

Dawn rose on the horizon in ribbons of scarlet and gray over London's Frost Faire. A blanket of fresh white snow had fallen last night and smothered the imperfections of the makeshift buildings and tents that crowded the shoreline and the frozen River Thames. Soon, a wide variety of shops would open, and street jugglers, acrobats and puppet shows would appear as though conjured from the crisp frigid air. The good people of London would swarm over the ice, enjoying the pleasures and entertainments.

But for Lady Elizabeth Montgomery, who sat astride her horse near the entrance of the tavern, the winter faire meant only the possibility of an end to her pain. The man who had murdered her fiancé, Donald, the Duke of Conclarton, was about to be captured and taken into custody. She had a choice to make. She could leave now and not confront Donald's murderer, or she could stay and face Lord Devonshire herself.

Her father and younger brother had told her that over a year spent mourning for Donald was admirable but it was high time she forgot him. They said Donald would have wanted her to marry and find happiness. But her beloved was dead and with him her dreams of a happily ever after.

How could her father and brother know that Donald would have wished that she marry, or know how long it took for a heart to heal? She could never forget Donald. Their marriage was to have been that rare thing in *ton* society—a love match. But it was more than that. Donald had encouraged her to train with him to become a code breaker and had been considering the prospect when he had been murdered.

She squared her shoulders, fighting the cold that seeped into her bones and tired muscles. She had forgotten the last time she had slept or eaten more than a few bites of food over the past few days. When she had learned of Devonshire's location, she and a contingency of soldiers had ridden through the night.

One of the officers, Captain Derek Fergus, approached her on horseback. He was an American in his early thirties, and a self-proclaimed adventurer who had fought in the Peninsular Wars. He had traveled with her since the incident with the runaway carriage and she found him a welcome distraction from her single-minded obsession to help bring her fiancé's murderer to justice.

Although well-spoken and very masculine in appearance, he was also the subject of unsavory gossip circling him like flies over rotting meat, so she had been cautioned.

The captain eased his horse next to hers, interrupting her thoughts. "Your ladyship, I received word that Devonshire is in custody and the men have matters well in hand. Justice has been served. Might I suggest we retire to an inn I spotted on our way here for a much-deserved meal?"

"Perhaps later," she said, her voice shaking. "There is something I need to deal with first. Justice will not bring Donald back from the dead, but my confronting Devonshire might end my nightmares."

Elizabeth dismounted on her own and marched toward the entrance to the makeshift tavern. Wind swirled around the entrance as guards escorted Devonshire forward in shackles. Defiant as ever, Devonshire protested that a man of his rank should not be treated so abominably.

She strode toward him, the disdain in his expression only fueling her determination. Her body trembled as her nails bit into the palms of her hands. She should ask Devonshire why he had killed Donald, but she already knew. Devonshire had meant to eliminate the heirs of the Conclarton dukedom, leaving himself the last in line. Money. Power. Greed. A deadly trifecta that had corrupted men and women for thousands of years.

Tears blurred her vision, but she swiped them away. "You took Donald from me, you miserable cur."

She doubled her fist and planted a facer with deadly accuracy.

Devonshire held his bloody nose and swore under his breath. Shouts to take him away and see to her care seemed to come from a great distance away. She swayed on her feet. It was over. Devonshire would be tried for his crimes. Imprisoned, likely hung. So why didn't she feel avenged? Why did her heart still ache?

She swayed on her feet again, and the torch lights around her dimmed. She was tired, so very tired. She longed for oblivion. The word sounded comforting. She ached for a great expanse of nothingness, where she could forget the pain, the loss, the heartache, if only for a short span of time. As her knees buckled, someone caught her in his arms. She thought it was the captain.

Chapter One

Three months later, March 1815

Lord Thomas Westerly had a choice to make. From his vantage point inside a stately residence, he allowed his thoughts to wander while he examined his options. Mayfair, London, in the grip of winter with its never-ending shades of gray, held a certain nostalgic appeal to him. Mayfair was where he had met his late wife. Their marriage had been brief, but it had produced a son, and for that he would be eternally grateful. His attention turned toward a fashionably dressed woman who had tilted her lovely head to gaze into the branches of a sycamore tree. Curious. The woman's sad expression seemed as conflicted as he felt.

February had been the month when, at ten years of age, he had been adopted from an orphanage. Twenty years later, he still wondered why the fates had abandoned him as a child and then chosen to rescue him when he was on the brink of turning to crime.

"I cannot change your mind, Lord Westerly? 'Tis a good offer." Dr. Merryweather said as he stood beside Thomas in the study. "It is a good offer, Lord Westerly. Although I must start calling you Dr. Westerly, of course." A portly gentleman, with a bush of white hair, and round, wire-rimmed spectacles, the good doctor reminded one of a kindly grandpapa more than a sawbones with an impeccable reputation in catering for the crème de la crème of London's *ton* society. "It is high time you remarried," he continued. "It has been three years since your wife's sudden death in childbirth. Your son Jonathan needs a mother, and I need a partner."

Thomas held his hands clasped tightly behind his back and faced the window overlooking a pedestrian walkway. "Jonathan lives with my wife's parents and is happy. I do not want to disrupt his life any more than it has already been. You sound like my aunt, Lady Tinsworthy, and I will say the same to you as I did to her. When, and if, I remarry is my own affair. As for your offer. I thank you, but it is not for me. I am keeping my promise to help my aunt and open a hospital in Merwood."

His old mentor had asked Thomas to join him in his practice, with the intent of taking it over when he retired. Thomas had other plans. He had vowed when he lived in the orphanage that he would help others regardless of their station in life. When Thomas had been adopted by the Earl of Willowdown, he had forgotten that vow, only to have it resurface when he had been bought a military commission. As an officer in the Peninsular Wars, he witnessed the cruelty of war and the difference in care officers received compared to infantry soldiers.

Dr. Merryweather leaned toward the window. "I say, why do you suppose one of my patients is climbing that old sycamore? Unseemly, particularly in her condition. You do not suppose she means to jump, do you?"

Thomas's eyebrows drew together as he whirled on the doctor. "Why would you say such a thing? Taking your own life is a desperate act."

"She is with child, unwed, and the father, an American military officer, has flown the coop, as it were. She mentioned that she wrote to him, but you know the sort. He is probably married with a dozen children. Pity. Her family is one of the oldest in London, and the scandal would cause quite a stir. I informed her about your aunt, Lady Tinsworthy, and the unwed mothers she cares for at Glen Castle, in Merwood, but she stormed out of here as though chased by banshees. Westerly! Where are you going?"

Halfway down the hall, Thomas turned toward the doctor. "What is your patient's name?"

"Lady Elizabeth Montgomery."

Thomas stormed outside and down the stairs. Would Lady Montgomery really harm herself and her unborn child rather than face the cut direct? But he knew from his time in the orphanage that it was a distinct possibility.

A crowd had gathered around the tree to gaze at the woman who, despite the fashionable red wool traveling coat and matching bonnet, had managed to climb two thirds of the way to the top. She had paused and was sitting on a wide branch, her back facing him, holding a conversation with herself. Was Merryweather correct? Had she gone mad?

A light drizzle had begun, which would make her descent slippery and more traitorous if she chose to change her mind and climb back down. Or perhaps she was resting while she gathered her courage to jump.

Either way, he could not stand here like a dolt.

"The devil," he said under his breath. There was nothing left to it. He would have to go after her. Doctor Merryweather had followed him outside and joined the increasing crowd of onlookers below the tree. Thomas handed him his hat and overcoat. "Wish me luck."

"You will need it. I have never known Lady Elizabeth to change her mind once it is set."

Thomas reached for a low-hanging branch and hauled himself up easily, putting his experience as a youth climbing trees to effective use. He moved with precision and stealth as he made his way toward the branch where Lady Montgomery sat with her slim, ramrod-straight back facing him. The last thing he wanted was to startle her.

The limb she had chosen was wide, but if she made a sudden movement she might slip from her perch and topple to the ground. The skirt of her rose-red dress had torn in the climb, and she had lost a shoe, exposing a shapely ankle, and leg.

As troubled as the lady's circumstances appeared, Thomas disagreed with Merryweather's assessment. Climbing a tree was an arduous task, more so when wearing a dress. If she meant to harm herself, why choose a tree when the top of a building would do?

But he could not take the chance that Merryweather *was* correct in his assessment.

He perched a short distance from her, close enough that he believed he could reach for her if she started to fall. "Fine day for a climb," he said, keeping his tone light.

Startled, she stiffened her spine, but remarkably kept her balance. She then turned her head in his direction. Her lovely silver eyes widened and deepened to a darker hue when she locked her gaze on him. And then he saw what he suspected was the real reason for the climb. She cradled a tabby kitten in her arms.

Relieved she had not meant to jump but rather to

rescue a stranded kitten, he let out a slow breath. Her motive for climbing the tree might be reckless, but he applauded its intent. Despite the cold and the beginning drops of what he assessed would be a roaring rainstorm, he smiled.

"Might I introduce myself? I am Lord Thomas Westerly but prefer to be addressed as Dr. Westerly."

Her eyes narrowed as she tilted her head. "Why are you here?"

She had not given her name, but *ton* propriety required an introduction by a third party before a lady offered her name to a man she had never met. He was not offended. Her voice held an edge of reproach which charmed him completely. If she had climbed to rescue the kitten, then he surmised she might have stayed to enjoy the quiet and tranquility the tree offered. He had spoiled it by entering her domain uninvited.

"I am here to save you, of course," he said.

Her lips edged at the corners in a smile. "My name is Lady Elizabeth Montgomery and I do not need saving." She looked toward the ground and the crowd. "I suppose Dr. Merryweather thought I might jump. How typical. And because I am with child, he sent you to fetch me."

"Actually, I volunteered. Now that I am here, I feel foolish. You clearly climbed the tree to rescue a kitten. That was brave."

"Why? Because I am a woman, and women do not or cannot climb trees?"

He shook his head, more to clear it of his growing admiration for this remarkable woman. She had confirmed that she was increasing and knew as an unwed mother she would face unspeakable cruelty, yet she had taken the time to help a kitten stranded in a tree. He leaned his head against the trunk of the tree. "On the contrary, you are brave because kittens have claws. I am not sure that I would have risked it."

Her smiled widened, and the beauty of it lit up her face as though rays of sunshine had escaped from behind the gray clouds. He was dazzled.

"All creatures respond to kindness," she said. "I have a feeling that you are the sort who brought home stray animals when you were a lad."

"Guilty as charged. Rescued animals make the best friends," he said, returning her smile.

She nuzzled the top of the kitten's head and was rewarded by a soft purr. Lady Montgomery's eyes sparkled with mischief. "We should climb down before the branch you are sitting on breaks. You are rather large to be climbing trees, you know."

He winked. "I am not worried. I have a feeling that if it breaks, you will save me." He held out his hand. "Shall we?"

****

The rain had been reduced to a soft gray mist as Thomas drew up his horse beside the Farrisworth House on Grosvenor Square. The inclement weather had kept traffic to a minimum. A half dozen couples, their identities hidden beneath umbrellas, hustled along the sidewalks to their destination while the occasional carriage pulled up alongside one of the houses.

Thomas dismounted, handing the ribbons to the groom, and took the stairs to the entrance to the elegant stone-and-brick Georgian house. He had neglected to send word to Viscount Farrisworth of his intention to pay a visit. That was not like him. The Lady Montgomery had been an unexpected distraction, and inexplicably he had found his thoughts turning to her from time to time. He had recommended she visit his aunt, but only time would tell if she heeded his advice. He reminded himself it was none of his affair.

Mr. Chesterfield opened the door. "Good day to you, Lord Westerly." The middle-aged butler had been in the viscount's service for a dozen or more years, and despite the reserved, pinched expression and soulful brown eyes, Chesterfield was a pleasant sort. "Do you prefer the title 'Doctor,' your lordship?"

"Doctor, if you please, Chesterfield. Are Lord and Lady Farrisworth accepting visitors today?"

"They noted your approach and are awaiting you with young Jonathan in the drawing room."

As he followed Chesterfield into the stately mansion, Thomas fingered in his pocket the toy horse he had made for Jonathan.

A two-year-old boy, with a mop of black curls and dancing hazel eyes, raced around the corner and rushed into Thomas's arms. He swept the boy up and swung him in a circle, laughing. "You have grown since I saw you last."

"Nonsense," an older woman said with a wide smile as she strolled toward him from around the same corner. "You only saw your son a week ago."

Thomas grinned back at the boy. "Your grandmama is wrong," he said to Jonathan. "You have grown taller."

"What did you bring me?" Jonathan said.

"Dearest," his grandmama said, rubbing the small of Jonathan's back, "your father does not always have to bring you a gift. It is gift enough that he can spare the time to see you."

Thomas set Jonathan on the floor and withdrew the toy from his pocket. "But I did bring you a gift. A wooden horse. Do you like it?"

"Very much."

"How long can you stay?" she said. "You know you are welcome as long as you like.

****

Across town, Elizabeth waited on the sidewalk outside Dr. Merryweather's office and handed him a letter as a carriage pulled into sight. "There is my carriage. If you would be so kind as to send this missive to my father."

A light drizzle of rain had begun again, and Dr. Merryweather opened his umbrella and held it over her head. "Dreadful day. I cannot persuade you to postpone your trip so that you can speak with your father yourself, Lady Elizabeth? His reaction might surprise you."

"And that would be my fondest wish. But now I cannot face him. He will be so disappointed in me. Besides, I went to the trouble to arrange that the carriage collect my luggage from the hotel and am anxious to be on my way. I have outlined in my letter where my father can find me if he so chooses. You are quite certain about Lady Tinsworthy?"

"Quite. She has never turned anyone away. With your approval, I will send a letter to her announcing when you might arrive."

She glanced down at her reticule. "Yes, I would like that very much. Dr. Westerly mentioned her to me as well. You mentioned that Lady Tinsworthy is Dr. Westerly's aunt and that she never married."

Dr. Merryweather held the umbrella over Elizabeth's head a little higher. "Never found the time, or so her nephew said. He calls her a force of nature."

"We are losing daylight, Dr. Merryweather. I should be on my way."

Dr. Merryweather helped her into the carriage and placed a blanket over her lap. "Safe journey."

Chapter Two

Merwood, England, one month later

Waves bellowed like thunder below Thomas's destination, the Glen Castle fortress in Merwood, as he rode his horse perilously close to the cliff's edge. He had received an urgent message that his aunt, Lady Tinsworthy, was ill and needed his care.

It had been a month since he had seen his aunt, and he chafed at his neglect. He would use the excuse that he was opening a hospital in the village. He could not tell her the real reason. She would laugh at the truth. He behaved like a schoolboy with his first crush. He could not purge the lovely tree-climbing Lady Montgomery from his thoughts.

He, of course, did not know if she had taken his and Dr. Merryweather's advice and come here to Glen Castle to ask for his aunt's help and shelter, but he had not wanted to take the chance.

Lady Montgomery was vulnerable, an unwed, expectant mother, in love with a man who had abandoned her. He could not fathom the pain or the strength it would take to make the tough decision she now faced. Hopefully, she had come here, as his aunt would help her as few could or would. But if Lady Montgomery were here, he would try to avoid her at all costs.

The roar of the ocean echoed like the cannons of Napoléon's armies that haunted his night terrors, barely drowning out his self-recriminations. The duties and challenges of running a hospital had taken him by surprise, as had the feelings for a woman he had barely exchanged more than a sentence or two. But that was a poor excuse. He must do more in the future to visit his aunt more often.

Reaching his destination, Thomas reined in his horse in the shadow of Glen Castle and dismounted in one fluid motion. Over the centuries, the castle had undergone countless transformations. Instead of a fortress prepared for attack, its occupants organized balls and soirees. In both instances there were winners and losers.

Giving instructions to the footman to care for his horse, Thomas grabbed his black leather bag and bounded up the stone entrance stairs two at a time. The urgent message he had received a short while ago had said it was a matter of life or death. No details of the injuries, just that it concerned his aunt. A twinge of guilt assaulted him again. If something had happened to her…

The butler, Mr. Fitzwilliam, a distinguished-looking older gentleman with wings of white hair at his temples, held the door open for him. Music and laughter assaulted Thomas's senses and chafed his nerves. He had no objection to either. He knew his aunt's purpose in hosting these events. But if his aunt was ill, why was there a party still in progress?

Fitzwilliam stepped aside to show Thomas into the entry. It was the middle of February, long past the Christmas Season, and yet his aunt continued to decorate as though her favorite time of the year was imminent. His aunt believed Christmas should be celebrated year-round.

Branches of lit candles reflected off a wall of mirrors and the polished twin staircase banisters in golden hues. White marble covered the entrance floor and glowed like a full moon in a cloudless sky. An ancient round oak table, dating back hundreds of years, stood in the center of the foyer. In its center a vase was filled with tree boughs, decorated with handmade green, red, and gold ornaments.

"My aunt?" Thomas inquired, taken back by how calmly Fitzwilliam was behaving. "Can you show me to her suite?"

"But of course, and it is a pleasure to see you again, sir. We have not seen you for a while. Your aunt will be pleased."

Thomas drew his eyebrows together. Fitzwilliam had sent him an urgent message regarding his aunt's health, written in the butler's own sprawling hand. Had Fitzwilliam grown forgetful and brain-fogged in his later years? Most men of Fitzwilliam's age retired to spend more time with their families. But Fitzwilliam had never married and was devoted to Thomas's aunt.

Thomas gentled his voice. "Fitzwilliam. You sent for me. Remember? Your missive claimed that my aunt's life was in peril. Or did I misread your intent?" Thomas knew that he had not misread the message, but he aimed to give the man a path to preserve his self-respect. A forgetful butler, no matter how revered, was not tolerated in *ton* society.

The butler nodded with a sigh. "You were not mistaken. In all the commotion it slipped my mind. I feared for Lady Tinsworthy, but thankfully, the crisis has been averted. She is entertaining a new guest in her suite and will be delighted to see you. Her ladyship was dancing when she received one of her attacks. She did not want to trouble you, but I thought it best to summon you as she was in such pain."

"You were wise to contact me. 'Twas no trouble."

The castle's Irish wolfhound bounded down the stairs and greeted Thomas with his customary loud bark. His aunt loved her dogs and went against convention, inviting them into her castle instead of banishing them outdoors to sleep in the stables. It was this shared trait that had brought them closer together when he had been adopted by her brother.

Thomas scratched the giant brindle behind the ear. "McDuff looks in a good mood, not his usual dire self. Fatherhood suits him."

"It does indeed," Fitzwilliam said with a slight smile. "It was a grand idea you had to breed McDuff with your brother's prize wolfhound—although the pups your aunt kept continue to race through the castle as though they, not your aunt, are its owners. They are a delight, but we must all be always on our guard."

Thomas's comment earlier to Fitzwilliam, that it had not been any trouble to drop everything and make a mad dash to Glen Castle, had been a colossal whopper. He had had to reschedule a surgery and beg a colleague to cover for him while he was away. His aunt had been more of a mother to him than an aunt, and he meant to assure that she lived as long as humanly possible.

Raised in an orphanage until he turned ten, Thomas had met Lady Tinsworthy when he had been adopted by her older brother, the Earl of Willowdown. His aunt had never married. She had said that she looked upon him as the child she had never had and insisted that Thomas call her Aunty Jessica. She had shown him kindness and acceptance when she might have treated him as an outsider.

The wolfhound walked in Thomas's wake as he followed Fitzwilliam to the suite on the second floor. With each step Thomas took, the music and laughter he had heard earlier grew softer.

His aunt had sent him an invitation to tonight's fete, but he had treated it as he had all the others. He had respectfully declined, citing his busy schedule at the hospital in Merwood as the reason, and then had thrown the invitation into the trash.

The primary reason for the balls she hosted every few months was matchmaking. London had its Season in the spring, with its grand marriage mart. His aunt's balls were year-round. Although her events were not entirely for Thomas's benefit, she had made it clear that, as her sole heir of Glen Castle, Thomas must marry. He had argued that marrying again was not for him. Her response had been: *We will see.*

Three of McDuff's gangly five-month-old puppies loped down the hallway, quickening their pace when they spied their papa. Describing the mass of fur and energy as mere *puppies* did not give an apt picture, though. They were already half the size of McDuff, who when he stood on his hind legs could rest his paws on Thomas's shoulders.

McDuff greeted his pups with a deep woof as they pounced on him with puppy enthusiasm. He licked them each in turn as they circled him, jumping to nip at his ears or bat their paws at his tail. Thomas picked up one of the playful pups and pulled another away from

McDuff, who seemed to gaze at Thomas with a silent thank-you.

Fitzwilliam hesitated at the entrance to the suite. "Although she will be pleased to see you, she will be cross with me for sending for you."

Thomas set the squirming pup down. He had known Fitzwilliam for as long as he had known his aunt and suspected that the man was half in love with his aunt. "Fear not, we will say that I was in the area and thought to stop by for a visit."

"At this late hour?"

"She is aware of my aversion to sleep and will not question the reason for my visit."

Fitzwilliam's expression erupted in a brief smile, which faded just as suddenly. "You are most kind, my lord." He knocked on one of the double doors, and on receiving permission to enter, he opened the door.

The wolfhound puppies squeezed past Thomas, tumbling over each other as they raced into the large room. His aunt had transformed one of the smaller upstairs ballrooms into her personal drawing room, connected to her bedchambers. The lofty ceilings were painted with murals depicting Artemis, the Greek goddess of the hunt, in a forest surrounded by animals and wildlife. Chairs and settees were grouped for conversation by windows or in front of twin fireplaces that were lit to chase away the chill air.

The puppies' destination was clear. Their keen smell had detected food. Thomas saw the disaster unfold before him as though in slow motion.

A petite, ebony-haired young woman, dressed too fashionably to be a servant, held a silver tray containing a pot of tea, teacups, and a two-tiered plate of assorted biscuits as she conversed with his aunt by a bank of windows.

He recognized her at once and caught his breath. She was Lady Montgomery, the very lady he had wanted to avoid. Dash it all, she looked lovelier in her green muslin dress overlaid with silver lace than he had remembered. So, she had taken his advice after all and contacted his aunt.

"Bloody hell," he said under his breath, then chastised himself for his selfish thoughts. It was not her fault he found her so attractive.

Well, done, Lady Montgomery, he amended. His aunt cared lovingly for unwed mothers, offering not only to care for them during their confinement but making sure each had a place to stay after the child was born. It was yet another reason his aunt was so dear to him.

A puppy barked, bringing Thomas back to the crisis at hand. He dropped his black bag and sprang forward as the swiftest of the teenage puppies reached Lady Montgomery. She turned to the side as the animal leapt, his paws landing on her back, nearly knocking her over. Teacups rattled on the tray and a lone cup and saucer landed on the floor, scattering its contents.

Saucer-eyed, she kept her balance as she braced for a second assault.

The remaining two puppies had reached their brother and, in tandem, all three lunged, knocking the tray from Lady Montgomery's grasp. Pottery crashed onto the carpet, spilling tea and scattering biscuits. The second impact caused her to lose her balance, but Thomas caught her in his arms before she fell.

"Stop at once," his aunt shouted to the puppies. "Naughty boys." But the puppies openly ignored her command, gobbled biscuits, and lapped up spilled tea.

"You, again," Lady Montgomery said with a smile, as their gazes locked.

"It would seem so," he said. He had picked her up in his arms to prevent her from falling when the puppies surged toward her. It was, of course, unnecessary. She was perfectly capable of standing on her own two feet once the lunge had accomplished its purpose. She leaned against him as though she belonged in his arms. Then, as though only just realizing she had leaned into him, she cleared her throat.

"I believe the danger has past, Lord Westerly," she said. "You can put me down now."

Reluctantly, he did as she asked and stepped back. "I apologize for the puppy's behavior, Lady Montgomery."

She waved his comment aside as she bent to rub one of the puppies behind his ear. "No need for an apology, my lord. They are acting like children, are they not, and must be forgiven their excitement. I cannot blame them. The biscuits are delicious." She tilted her head to look over and smile at him. It radiated light and warmth as it had when he had climbed the tree to help her down. He could stand here forever, basking in that smile.

Her hair had remained in its severely coiled bun at the nape of her neck, and her dress looked only slightly rumpled. She looked every inch the lady. But there was also a warm femininity, and a gentleness of nature that contradicted the primness of her appearance. The contradiction was intriguing.

Fitzwilliam rushed to gather the puppies, calling them by name and attempting to pull them from their feast. Thomas jumped into the fray, and two footmen appeared on the scene with offers of help. Together the four men managed to corral and then coax the three exuberant troublemakers toward the exit.

Thomas, wrestling for control with the most energetic of the pups, glanced over his shoulder toward Lady Montgomery. She was conversing with his aunt as though they were old friends.

In the instant he took to look away, the puppy seized his opportunity and broke free. Thomas sprang to his feet and leapt upon the renegade, tackling him to the ground. His brothers had also escaped and joined in the playful wrestling, licking Thomas's face.

From the bank of windows, he heard laughter. Lady Montgomery was gazing over at him, her eyes lit in merriment as she laughed again. Absently, he knew his clothes would be covered in puppy drool. He did not care. It was worth it to see her smile.

Chapter Three

A mere hour later, quiet and order had been restored in Lady Tinsworthy's suite. The puppies had been successfully removed, the mess they had created had been cleaned away, and a fresh pot of tea had been delivered, along with biscuits and jam. Elizabeth wished the puppies had been allowed to stay and would suggest the notion to Lady Tinsworthy in the future. Animals, Elizabeth had learned, even those as exuberant as puppies, had an amazing capacity to help bring calm and love to those around them. She was glad Lady Tinsworthy allowed them into her home.

Elizabeth sat in an oversized wingback chair, reading Jane Austen's novel *Emma* to Lady Tinsworthy, whose leg was propped on a cushioned footstool as she sipped an amber liquid from a sherry glass. It was clear to Elizabeth that her ladyship suffered from gout, a condition that had also plagued her father. Night air and its chill had descended, and Elizabeth and Lady Tinsworthy had moved from the windows to sit opposite each other by a cozy fire.

Elizabeth paused in her reading to smooth her dress where the puppy who had jumped on her earlier had snagged a thread. She would have to have it repaired. It was by no means her favorite, but the damage had been done. No matter. It had been an accident. She had planned to add another panel or two to this one to accommodate her expanding waistline.

She still found it difficult to believe that she was with child. She had not felt the babe inside her move yet, but Lady Tinsworthy assured her that it was too early. Some mornings, Elizabeth awoke and for a moment believed it had been all a dream. How could she have had such a lapse in judgment as to sleep with a man she barely knew?

Working to prove that Devonshire had killed her fiancé had consumed every waking hour and kept at bay her profound grief over Donald's death. In a blink, Devonshire was in custody and her life no longer held purpose. She felt adrift. The captain's soothing, love-filled words were a balm to her broken heart. But she could not blame him. She knew what she was doing. Part of her realized that his words held a false ring, as though he had said them to vulnerable women before. She wanted to block out the pain if only for a short time.

She was unwed, the whereabouts of the father of her child unknown, and she had limited resources.

When her mother had died giving birth to Elizabeth's brother, she had left Elizabeth a small inheritance. Elizabeth was uncertain what arrangements her father would make for her when he learned of her condition, and so that inheritance would have to suffice.

Thankfully, she had met Lord Westerly in London and he had followed up Dr. Merryweather's recommendation by telling her more about Lady Tinsworthy and her generosity in helping ladies, such as Elizabeth. Lady Tinsworthy called them her Ladies in Waiting, and for each one found a suitable husband, or a good family for the child, or a respectable position where she could afford to raise her child on her own.

When Elizabeth met her ladyship, she suggested the marriage option as the most advantageous. Elizabeth was less certain. What man would marry a woman of limited resources and with a child born out of wedlock? That left her wondering about the other two options.

The faint echo of music drifted from the ballroom downstairs, interrupting her train of thought. The ball had continued as though nothing untoward had occurred. Lady Tinsworthy would have had it no other way. There was a purpose for the gathering, and she had given instructions that nothing should stand in the way. Her ladyship considered her matchmaking balls on par with those conducted in London.

Unlike the *ton* events in London, however, Lady Tinsworthy did not consider a person's title or wealth when extending an invitation. A person's good character, ability to provide a loving home, and sincere intention of marrying gained them entrance.

Upon arriving, Elizabeth attended three or four such balls and entertainments. They were exhausting and Elizabeth begged for a pause. Was her aversion to finding a husband because she was still in love with Donald? Or just the dream of what she envisioned their life together would be?

Her fiancé's death haunted her still. Her only consolation was that his killer had been brought to justice. She knew that she would always love Donald, but the pain of that loss had driven her to do something foolish and very unlike herself. She had engaged in an affair with a man of dubious character. Every man she had loved—or thought she had loved—had either died or betrayed her. She must guard her heart against romantic love.

"Are feeling unwell?" Her ladyship cleared her throat raised her long-handled, gold-and-diamond-encrusted lorgnette to her eyes. "You look a little pale. We could continue at another time."

In her late fifties, Lady Tinsworthy still retained a youthful appearance. She wore a silk dress with shades of amber and gold over her matronly frame. The dress brought out the copper highlights in her hazel green eyes. Her hair was braided and coiled like a crown on the top of her head. It shone like brushed silver in the light from the branch of candles on the table beside a cluster of amber-colored glass bottles. Elizabeth had asked her once why she had never married, but she had changed the subject. Glen Castle, it seemed, was a place that loved its secrets.

"My apologies, Lady Tinsworthy. "It would seem I am traveling in my own thoughts. Emma and her exploits will be a welcome distraction."

Lady Tinsworthy reached over to pat Elizabeht's hand. "Have no fear. You will be well taken care of and surrounded by love. If you have lost your place, Mr. Knightley was preparing to dine with Emma after their disagreement."

"Chapter Twelve. Right you are." Elizabeth resumed where she had left off in the story. The character Emma was a highborn lady who considered herself a matchmaker of sorts, not unlike Lady Tinsworthy. But unlike her ladyship, Emma's interference in the lives of her friends was not always welcome. As the chapter opened Mr. Knightley had planned to dine with Emma. There was a smudge line under the word 'invitation,' indicating that the ink had not dried properly.

The release date for Jane Austen's novel had been

scheduled for this coming December during the Christmas season, but her ladyship had secured an advance copy of *Emma*. Elizabeth had been stunned that her ladyship had managed to obtain the coveted title. When questioned, Lady Tinsworthy refused to disclose the identity of the person who had obtained the novel. Elizabeth had learned that her ladyship's outspoken circle of bluestocking friends and influential contacts extended far and wide, and she guarded their identities as fiercely as McDuff protected his pups, or her fiancé his secrets when he worked for the Crown.

Donald had often talked to her regarding the possibility of joining him in his work. He said she would be invaluable in helping him develop a Book Cipher based on the Jane Austin novels. He theorized that no one would suspect novels read primarily by women would contain secret messages and words with double meanings. His idea was intriguing, but of course utter nonsense. She would soon be a mother and was content to discover new novels. And her favorites were those written by Jane Austen.

Elizabeth adored every novel Austen had written and had shared her enthusiasm for the stories with Lady Tinsworthy's Ladies In Waiting. Counting herself, there were currently a total of five ladies residing at Glen Castle. Three of them were attending the ball this evening, and the fourth was resting—her child was expected any day.

Then there was Lord Westerly.

Elizabeth had a vivid memory of the man. He had climbed the oak tree, unmindful of the rain, believing only that she needed rescuing, and he was the man for the job. His voice had been gentle when he spoke but contained a quiet strength. He was undeniably handsome. But she had met handsome men. So, what was it about him that made his mere presence coax her into a smile?

The man was unlike any physician she had ever met. The physical appearance of most doctors reminded Elizabeth of a plump porkpie or Christmas pudding. Their complexions were sallow and pale—from spending too much time indoors, she supposed—and their general demeanor pompous. They believed themselves experts and their decisions on how to treat a patient beyond reproach.

He had a square jawline, and his sun- and wind-bronzed face displayed a diagonal scar from his hairline down the left side of his face. A scar that instead of marring his appearance only enhanced it. When the puppies had burst into Lady Tinsworthy's suites, causing her to lose her balance, he had picked her up as though she weighed no more than feathers, and she had felt the muscles in his powerful arms and his solid chest.

Her interest in him took her off guard. She should focus and not allow such an inconvenient distraction. Lady Tinsworthy took care of everyone around her, but who looked after her? The least Elizabeth could do was to assure herself that Dr. Westerly was competent.

For example, had he even attended medical school? It was common for gentlemen to simply declare themselves doctors, set up a shingle, and opened their doors for business. And did he understand that administering to the health of a woman was different from that of a man?

The more she thought about Dr. Westerly the more frustrated she became. It was widely accepted that doctors would experiment on patients if they did not know the cause of their illness.

"I say, Lady Elizabeth," Lady Tinsworthy said, raising her lorgnette again. "What has you so distracted? You have reread the passage where the reader first meets Emma and Mr. Knightley at least three times. In the passage Emma tells her father that the gentleman in question always finds fault with her."

Elizabeth settled a ribbon in the book to hold her place. "If you would indulge me, could you enlighten me regarding Dr. Westerly? I will be honest. He does not have the look of a physician or surgeon. He looks genuinely like a military man, a captain or colonel. But if that were the case, he would demand that we address him using that designation or that of his title, and yet you have said that he expressly wishes to be addressed as Doctor Westerly. Did he attend medical school, for example? Who recommended him?"

Her ladyship sipped from her crystal sherry glass, a half-smile lifting the corners of her mouth. "I daresay my nephew made quite the impression. You are a very perceptive young woman. He was indeed in the military."

"Your nephew? I…"

Her ladyship lifted a staying hand. "At my suggestion, my brother adopted Thomas when he was ten years old. My brother and his wife had only one child, a son, and were unable to have more children. At my insistence, I suggested that they adopt. It is all well and good to have an heir, but my brother's holdings were substantial. I told him that he would be wise to also have a spare lest, God forbid, something happened to his only son and all his wealth went to a distant cousin."

A thunderous bark broke into the tranquil silence as Dr. Westerly entered the room with one of the wolfhound puppies trotting at his side.

"Ah, here is the child of my heart now." Lady Tinsworthy held out her arms toward Dr. Westerly. "We were just talking about you. It took you a dreadfully long time to return. What kept you? And before you answer, you must know that Lady Elizabeth doubts that you attended medical school," she said with a twinkle in her eye. "Lady Elizabeth wants to assure that I am in the best of care."

Dr. Westerly reached for his aunt's hands and bent to kiss her on the cheek. "I apologize for my tardiness. Your wolfhound puppies gave me little choice. I had to change or embarrass you dreadfully. My clothes were soaked through to the bone with their puppy kisses. The little hooligans delighted in licking and drooling all over me."

Elizabethe ducked her head to hide her smile, placing the Austen novel on her lap. He had a gentle way with animals that she heartily approved of, but she must not let that dissuade her from determining if he was qualified to administer to Lady Tinsworthy. Elizabeth had grown quite fond of her ladyship over a short span of time. She must never forget that her mother had died in childbirth due to the incompetence of her attending physician.

Lady Tinsworthy patted the doctor's hand. "You are forgiven. Lady Elizabeth mentioned that the two of you met in London and that I have you to thank for convincing her to visit me at Glen Castle. But I am old-fashioned and believe a formal introduction is in order. Lady Montgomery, I would like to introduce you to my nephew, Viscount Westerly or, as he prefers, Doctor Thomas Westerly."

Dr. Westerly made Elizabeth a bow as the wolfhound puppy trotted toward his aunt and plopped down at her feet. "It is my pleasure to meet you again, Lady Montgomery," Dr. Westerly said, his eyes holding hers for a moment that quickened her pulse. He was too good-looking to be a physician. It was disconcerting.

His aunt offered the wolfhound puppy a biscuit that he gobbled in one bite. "I commend you, Thomas. Finnigan is much improved. How ever did you persuade him to behave?"

Dr. Westerly scratched Finnigan behind his ear. "I merely told him that it was not gentlemanly to pounce on a lady. Lady Montgomery," he said, turning toward her, "if I may assuage your concerns regarding administering to my aunt, I did indeed graduate from medical school. After selling my commission in the military, I attended Cambridge and Guy's Medical Hospital in Southwick. Guy's Hospital is near Shakespeare's Globe Theater and is the oldest university in the world."

Impressive, she considered to herself, but she must continue. "But did you finish your studies and graduate, or merely attend for one or two years, as the poet Keats was reported to have done? Please excuse my skepticism, sir. You are the nephew of Lady Tinsworthy, your father is, or was, the Earl of Willowdown, and your brother the current earl. Your aunt introduced you as Viscount Westerly. Sons of noble families, even those who are adopted, if they are not the heir, choose the military, the church, or the bar as their occupation. Or they content themselves with living off their estates or their family's wealth. They rarely become physicians."

Doctor Westerly had not moved and yet his stance looked relaxed and at ease. It appeared that for all her penetrating questions he had not taken offense.

He stole a glance toward his aunt, who idly stroked Finnegan's head, and returned to focus on Lady Montgomery. "I wish more people were like you," he said, "and questioned those who tended to their care. I received my medical degree from Cambridge and became a Fellow of the Royal College of Physicians."

Elizabeth nodded slowly, stealing a glance toward her ladyship. His aunt had remained uncharacteristically quiet throughout Elizabeth's exchange with her nephew. Only those who had graduated from Oxford and Cambridge could become a Fellow of the Royal College of Physicians. It was a high honor, and its physicians were granted fellowships rather than just licenses. Members of this select group were often called upon to administer to the nobility and even the royal family. But why had he chosen this small coastal village? To make sure he was closer to his aunt.

She pressed her lips together. The man was impossible to dislike. He was intelligent, kind, and maddeningly handsome.

Finnigan chose that moment to leave Lady Tinsworthy and ambled over toward Elizabeth. He nudged her hand with his wet nose. His big soulful brown eyes gazed toward her as though he wanted her to pet him.

She smiled, obliging willingly. The animal sensed her predicament and offered a calming presence. She was the guest of Lady Tinsworthy and was interrogating her beloved nephew on his medical credentials. What was wrong with her? Why was she trying so hard to find fault with the man? This was not like her. She had learned that ladies in the family way were prone to emotional turbulence. Was that the reason for her critical and judgmental mood? Or was something else at play? She should leave before she made a further cake of herself.

"Dr. Westerly, you have impressive credentials. Thank you for graciously answering all my questions. With your permission, your ladyship, I believe I will take my leave."

"By all means," Lady Tinsworthy said. "But won't you reconsider attending tonight's festivities? I had a lovely silk dress set aside for you in your room. There are gentlemen who have made inquiries about you."

Elizabeth bent to kiss Lady Tinsworthy on the cheek. "You are kindness itself, but I fear the gentlemen expect a rich dowry to accompany my title, and I am without one."

"You have not spoken with your father, then?" Lady Tinsworthy pursed her lips. "Forgive me. It was not my place to ask. But very few of my ladies have dowries and fewer still possess a title as lofty as yours. Besides, I seek love matches for you all, not business arrangements. I will not pressure you, however."

Elizabeth held the Jane Austen novel against her bosom. With each month that passed, the babe inside her grew, and her belly increased. Time for her was running out. She must wed before her child was born or give the babe up for adoption. But a love match? She had loved once and then had given in to weakness to lie with a man who professed to love her. She no longer had confidence in the word.

She forced a smile. "You are kind to remind me of

the interested gentlemen. Please give them my regards, but I have never been one to enjoy dancing." She paused. "The hour is late, your ladyship. Would you mind if I bid you goodnight?"

"Of course, dear. And I will take into consideration your aversion to dancing when I plan my next entertainments. We will have a number of summer gatherings but must start planning for our Christmas Ball. It is by far my most successful matchmaking ball." She pointed her lorgnette toward her nephew. "Dr. Westerly will attend as well."

"I will not," he growled. "We have discussed the matter."

"My boy, I do not listen to topics you discuss, particularly when your opinions run contrary to my own. I will have a ball and you will attend. You need a wife. Lady Elizabeth needs a husband."

"Lady Tinsworthy," Elizabeth said, pressing the novel to her bosom, "you cannot suggest…"

"Yes, she can," Dr. Westerly said, turning toward his aunt. "Aunt, I know what you suggest. I will not have you selecting my bride. Lady Elizabeth and I are not suited."

"Of course. The two of you a match? What gave you both such a preposterous notion?" She nodded toward Elizabeth. "Have a pleasant evening, my dear."

Chapter Four

Thomas waited until Lady Montgomery had closed the door behind her. The lady was still as outspoken and lovely as the first moment they had met. He clasped his hands behind his back. "Extraordinary."

The lady defied the portrait of a docile *ton* woman, she spoke her mind, questioned his medical credentials, and had an affection toward animals. A love of animals was not unusual. But how many women of her station would risk not only life and limb but a fashionable dress to climb a tree to rescue a kitten? Or not descend into hysterics when puppies slobbered over their clothes?

No, he stood by his assessment. Lady Montgomery was extraordinary indeed.

The room had chilled, and he bent to stoke the coals in the fireplace while he pondered her. He had encountered women who spoke their minds before. His aunt, for one, then surrounded herself with like-minded Bluestockings. He felt grateful Lady Montgomery had taken his advice to visit his aunt. Life was unforgiving to women who found themselves in Lady Montgomery's situation: pregnant and unwed.

"Indeed, she is extraordinary," his aunt said, taking another sip from her sherry glass and breaching into his thoughts. "Have you spoken with your brother lately?"

He dusted off his hands and moved to examine the collection of bottles containing amber liquid on the table near his aunt. It was so like his aunt to mention his brother, Harry, whenever the two of them were together. She believed in the importance of family and openly disapproved of the rift that continued to grow unchecked between him and his brother.

"He harbors a deep-seated hatred toward me," Thomas said. "I married the woman he loved."

"It is more than that. Besides, you did not know that he loved Sarah when you offered marriage." She held out her hand toward him to draw him toward her. "But you must try. Harry is a troubled young man. The death of his father, may my brother rest in peace, made Harry the Earl of Willowdown, and with it came the responsibilities *and* your father's demons. My brother disapproved of my inheriting Glen Castle unentailed and condemned my offering aid and comfort to my Ladies in Waiting. My brother believed it a scandal that I harbored such women. Harry means to accomplish what his father failed to do: force me to abandon what has been my life's work to help others. His latest ploy is to try and hire my servants away."

"His plan will fail," Thomas said. "You would merely hire more. Is he aware that your wealth exceeds his?"

"He is not, and I wish to keep it our secret. It would only promote a deeper chasm between you and your brother. Misunderstandings between family and friends are like an infestation of weeds. The longer they have time to grow and set down deep roots, the more difficult it is to reverse the damage. The two of you must find a path forward. His childish attempt to hire my servants might prove an excuse for the two of you to open a dialogue."

"You are right."

She settled back against the cushions and cast him a lopsided grin. "I usually am. Lady Elizabeth is a little slip of a thing but in possession of a great deal of unrealized strength. I daresay you made quite the impression on her. I have never seen her quite so animated."

"We have returned to matchmaking, then? I was hopeful you had forgotten." He returned the cork to the bottle of amber liquid he had been examining.

"Silly boy, I thought you knew me better."

"We have debated this topic before. I am not prepared to remarry, especially to someone like Lady Montgomery. The woman would challenge me at every turn," he said, then to himself adding *and is dangerously lovely*. A man could lose all sense of reason with a woman like the Lady Montgomery.

"You have forced the role of matchmaker upon me. I have declared you my heir to Glen Castle and all my holdings, and out of compassion, I gave you time to grieve your wife's death. But it has been three years and you have given me little recourse. Your son, Jonathan, needs his father, and I need you to find a wife and produce male children so that my property is secured."

Thomas gazed at the rolling flames. "Jonathan is better off with my wife's family. Regarding my setting up a nursery again, I have time."

"I disagree. You of all people know how precarious life is. None of us knows how much time we have left on this earth. I know you carry the weight of your wife's death on your shoulders, but it was not your fault. You were not even there when she went into labor. You must stop blaming yourself."

But the fact that he was not at his wife's bedside when she went into labor laid the foundation for his guilt. "I can find my own wife."

"Clearly, you cannot."

He turned the bottle he had recorked. The label read, *Dr. Gordon's Gout Tincture.* The liquid reeked of alcohol, honey, and cloves. When he set the bottle down, he noticed a small round canister. At first, he thought his aunt had begun using snuff, but on closer examination, he realized it was crushed tea leaves. He smelled the contents, identifying the pungent smell of white willow bark tea. There was a robust debate in the medical community regarding this tea. Some argued that it eased the symptoms of gout, while others claimed that it worsened the condition. Thomas intended to proceed with caution until more information was gathered.

"Instead of consulting me," he said, setting the tea aside, "you are taking matters into your own hands and choosing medicines that are worthless. Fitzwilliam should have consulted me before providing you with medicine. The contents in this bottle you are drinking are nothing more than sweetened brandy. And as for the tea—"

"You have changed the subject."

"I have learned from the best. You must stop drinking the tincture at once. We can discuss the tea later." He held out his hand, indicating her glass.

She snorted, handing him her half empty glass. "As you can see, I am much improved."

He set her glass on the table. "You feel better because you have had two or three glasses of brandy, and the alcohol has numbed the pain. Until you change the number of sweets you eat, your condition will not improve. This is a serious matter. No wonder Fitzwilliam sent me an urgent message. You should have told me your gout had worsened."

"Mr. Fitzwilliam is nothing but an old worrywart. I concede that, at my suggestion, he purchased the tinctures, but Lady Elizabeth provided the white willow bark tea. She had brewed more of the tea when the puppies burst in, causing a commotion. She said that her father is afflicted with gout and the tea eases his pain."

He let out his breath slowly and took another breath before he commented. He was pleased that Lady Montgomery's father had found relief with the tea, but that was not enough to dissuade him. His aunt was too willing to try the latest remedy despite his constant warnings. She took too many chances with her health.

"Promise me that you will consult with me on matters of your health. For example, what were you thinking to host a ball when you were not feeling well?"

"How else will my Ladies in Waiting find suitable husbands? My ladies do not have an endless supply of time to find someone. I cannot allow my own discomfort to prevent them from finding their happily ever after." His aunt folded her hands in her lap. "I know you are looking out for my welfare, but my ladies are important to me, and at times you behave more like you are still in the military issuing orders rather than that sweet, kind little boy who was always bringing home stray animals. I never should have bought you a commission."

He took her hands in his. "I apologize. We will figure out a compromise. And you bought me a commission because I begged for one. You knew as well as I that I did not belong here. And it was you who taught me to protect those who were defenseless…or stubborn," he said with a wink.

She reached over and squeezed his hand. "You *do* belong here. Never doubt that. But what am I to do with you? You need a wife."

"I know."

Chapter Five

The faint sound of music that Elizabeth had heard earlier was but a distant memory as she left Lady Tinsworthy and made her way down the well-lit hallway toward the wing that housed Lady Tinsworthy's Ladies in Waiting. There was sadness in the quiet. While the music had continued, she had considered participating. She had not been truthful when she told her ladyship she did not like to dance.

She loved dancing.

It was everything else about balls that she loathed. A lady must dazzle in both appearance and clever conversation. She must not laugh too loudly, show enthusiasm while dancing, or distress if she was a wallflower. Her sole purpose was to attract a husband. Dash it all—and dash Dr. Westerly for looking so handsome and broad-shouldered, with hands so large she knew his would engulf hers. What would dancing with him be like? She pressed her hand against the flutter in her stomach and pressed her lips together. She was behaving like a silly schoolgirl.

She rounded a corner and headed down a long hallway. Sconces hung from the walls, their light casting a gentle glow over groupings of polished tables and vases filled with greenery.

She estimated that it was well past midnight, the time in London when balls were at their height. In the country, however, people went home early. But although the guests had left for their homes, or retired to their rooms, she knew the ladies in the east wing would be awake.

She held a single candle in one hand and the Austen novel in the other as she approached the doors leading to their drawing room. The hallway on either side of the suite was as bright as during the day. Her ladyship's standing order was that the sconces and branches of candles on the tables were maintained twenty-four hours a day for the safety of the women in her charge who might need to leave their rooms in the middle of the night.

She entered and once again was struck by the detailed care Lady Tinsworthy took with everything that touched her ladies.

The suite of rooms was decidedly feminine. Murals of goddesses from mythology were painted on the high ceilings and restful scenes of meadows bursting with spring flowers spread over the walls. Fabrics covering stuffed chairs and sofas were in an assortment of colors of the rainbow. It was a happy room, full of sunshine, designed to chase away even the gloomiest of days.

Laughter and a hum of conversation layered over a rustle of skirts as a trio of young women, brightly dressed in pink, yellow, and springtime blue, strolled in from an adjoining room. Miss Coalton, Miss Brown, and Mrs. Neverly were in various stages of their pregnancy. It was apparent, from the gowns they wore, that they had attended the ball earlier in the evening. Their eyes lit like stars as they saw the sumptuous food displayed on a side buffet table.

"Splendid!" Mrs. Neverly said. "Lady Elizabeth, we

are pleased you have arrived. We have much to tell you. Miss Coalton was a sensation, and we expect one of the gentlemen will offer for her soon. Miss Brown secured a position as a servant with Merwood's vicar and his wife…and you have brought Jane Austen's book to read to us. How wonderful!"

"Please join us, Lady Elizabeth," Miss Coalton, said, waving her over to the buffet table as she tossed back her blonde curls and poured herself a cup of tea. "I feel as sick as a cushion. I cannot eat nothin' that doesna come right back up again, but it is generous of her ladyship to provide this for the rest of us." Miss Coalton had arrived a sennight after Elizabeth and had kept the circumstances revolving around her pregnancy a secret.

Mrs. Neverly, in her twenties, a lovely woman with striking red hair, reached for a plate beside a bowl of boiled eggs. "Well, I am famished. You will get your appetite back, Miss Coalton," Mrs. Neverly said with a smile. "The first few months are the worst of it. Lady Elizabeth, we heard you met Dr. Thomas Westerly. Now, there is a man who would make even the strongest of us swoon."

Miss Brown eased herself down on a chair, ignoring the food. She rubbed her belly, letting out her breath. "Oh, that last one was a strong one." She looked like she was due to give birth any day. She had worked as a chambermaid at one of the estates inland. The son of the manor's lord had forced himself upon her, and when he learned she was carrying his child, he had had her dismissed. "Dr. Westerly cares about 'is patents, 'e does," Miss Brown continued. "Saved my brother's legs from amputation when others thought to chop them off."

Elizabeth poured a cup of tea for Mrs. Neverly, then

for herself. Yet another good accounting of Dr. Westerly. "I have heard you mention your brother before," Elizabeth said. "He fought in the Peninsular Wars, did he not?"

Miss Brown rubbed her belly again. "I am as fat as a cow and this babe kicks night and day. The monthly nurse insists it is time for my lying-in to begin. I told her I was not ready. But you asked about my brother. 'Tis true that a cannon explosion nearly shattered his legs, but 'e was brought here to Merwood for care and that is where 'e met Dr. Westerly. The good doctor runs a small hospital in the village." She closed her eyes, pressing her lips together.

Mrs. Neverly set her cup down to take Miss Brown's hand in hers. "That is enough talking, Miss Brown. You need to rest and build your strength. Lady Elizabeth will kindly read us a few chapters to settle our minds for a good night's sleep."

Elizabeth nodded, exchanging a glance with Mrs. Neverly before she began. Elizabeth had noticed Mrs. Neverly's worried expression. But Elizabeth had been mistaken. It had been a long day for them all. She opened Austen's novel to where she had left off reading to them last evening.

Chapter Six

The next morning, Elizabeth stood as still as a statue in the dining room before windows that framed the castle's vegetable garden. Mrs. Neverly and Miss Coalton were already in the dining room enjoying their breakfast. Outside, green sprouts pushed their way through the earth, promising an end to the dreary winter months. It had been a restless night.

She brought her rose-colored shawl more tightly about her shoulders. The very thought of strolling along a path, without a care in the world, as she had done before her world had been turned upside down, seemed a welcomed gift. But the air was damp and rain clouds formed overhead, a reminder that winter had not relaxed its hold just yet.

She had read to the ladies longer than she had anticipated. Everyone was on edge, knowing that Miss Brown's babe might be born at any time. It was bittersweet. They openly rejoiced in the birth of the child yet kept to themselves the reality that Miss Brown intended on giving her child up for adoption. Elizabeth's own thoughts on the matter had resulted in a sleepless night. She would face the same decision when it was time for her child to be born.

Inside the dining room, servants brought platters of breakfast foods, both savory and sweet, as well as tea and coffee. Elizabeth had never heard of Lady Tinsworthy before Dr. Merryweather and Dr. Westerly had mentioned her name, both on the same day. She had learned that her ladyship employed an accoucheur, who was a man-midwife, and a monthly nurse and wet nurse. Elizabeth could not imagine a more generous and kinder woman. Whatever the outcome, she was grateful she was here in Merwood and not in London under her father and the *ton*'s judgmental stare.

She rested her hand on her slightly rounded belly. Sometime in the middle of the night she felt the babe growing inside her move. The joy that had accompanied that moment had taken her by surprise, as did the sudden warmth that had embraced her heart. Then, as the babe's movement subsided, the wave of uncertainty took its place. As an unwed mother, the logical recourse was to give her child up for adoption as Miss Brown planned to do. The mere thought chilled her to the bone. Would she have the strength to do it?

Elizabeth had intended to wait until Lady Tinsworthy arrived, but her stomach growled so loudly it brought a smile from Mrs. Neverly. No one criticized Elizabeth for the size of her portions of food at Glen Castle. In fact, she was encouraged to eat and build up her strength. Her ladyship was a believer that a robust appetite helped promote health in both the mother and the child she carried. In London, a woman's appearance was more important than her health, and gaining weight during confinement had been frowned upon.

Lady Tinsworthy bustled into the dining room, her face flushed, and her expression pinched with concern. "Miss Brown has been brought into the lying-in room."

Mrs. Neverly and Miss Coalton were on their feet in an instant.

"What can we do?" Mrs. Neverly said.

"We are to remain calm and continue as we have," Lady Tinsworthy said. "I am informed that everything is well in hand. Dr. Westerly joined the accoucheur, Mr. Wentworth, and the monthly nurse, Mrs. Morris, and offered his assistance. Miss Brown is in good hands."

Elizabeth pushed her plate aside. She was too young when her brother was born to remember that night. She did remember that for years afterward her father said he wished he had been allowed into the lying-in room. It may not have had influence in the outcome, he argued, but the thought of his wife without those who loved her had always haunted him.

"I disagree," Elizabeth said, standing. "I am sure that Miss Brown would like her friends with her. Not all of us at once. We could take turns."

"Splendid idea," Mrs. Neverly said as Miss Coalton bobbed her head in agreement. "Lady Elizabeth can read, I can hold Miss Brown's hand, and Miss Coalton has a lovely voice."

Lady Tinsworthy swiped at a tear. "You ladies warm my heart. It is indeed a splendid idea. Come along. I expect us to meet with sound disagreement, but it has been my experience that numerous and consistent voices can topple even the fiercest obstacles."

****

A few hours later a beautiful baby girl was born. Elizabeth held the swaddled baby girl in her arms, rocking back and forth slowly. She had followed Lady Tinsworthy to the drawing room. It was universally declared that Miss Brown had an easy birth, and when Dr. Westerly announced that indeed her friends had helped keep Miss Brown peaceful and calm during the labor, Mr. Wentworth had begrudgingly concurred.

"The child is a lovely girl," she said to the couple striding into the room beside her.

The middle-aged couple were not fashionably dressed in the latest finery, but their clothes were smart and well-tailored in shades of navy blue and emerald, green. Her ladyship had mentioned that she had known the couple for some time. They owned a farm near to Glen Castle but had not been blessed with a child of their own.

The woman's expression broke out in smiles as she pressed her hands against her bosom. "Is it true, Harold? Are we to have a child after all these years?"

Harold put his arm around his wife. "Only if you wish it, Mary my love."

"Oh, yes! A baby girl… Can you imagine it, Harold? A child after all these years! We are so blessed. I mean to spoil her beyond measure."

Harold smiled, kissing his wife on the forehead. "I would have it no other way, my love."

With a nod from Lady Tinsworthy, Elizabeth brought the child over to Mary and Harold.

Elizabeth did cry, then. Not the sobbing sort, with great sighs, and moans, but the quiet kind. Tears traveled silently down her checks, one landing on the child's blanket as she placed the babe into Mary's arms. Miss Brown must have been in such emotional pain, knowing she had to give up her child. The tears were for Miss Brown, and for herself and all the women who had to make the same choice. The pain must have been unbearable.

Lady Tinsworthy linked her arm through Elizabeth's as though sensing her thoughts. "This is a bittersweet day."

Elizabeth blinked, raising her chin. "You must find something for me to do. Something that keeps both mind and body active."

Her ladyship nodded slowly. "I have just the thing. Dr. Westerly needs help. He will not admit it to me, of course. As you have learned, he opened a hospital in Merwood. The poor man thinks he can be both the head doctor and its administrator. Would you consider assisting him?"

"I have no background in running a hospital."

"You are intelligent, have a curious and open mind, and are not afraid to question what you do not understand. I have little doubt that you are exactly what my nephew needs."

Chapter Seven

After the long gray months of winter, the first days of April brought sunshine and the promise of spring as the carriage rumbled along the ten-mile journey from Glen Castle to the village of Merwood. The hum of conversation inside had subsided as Elizabeth gazed out the carriage window. Everywhere she looked there were signs of spring to quiet her growing trepidations.

Violets and yellow kingcup flowers spread over fields and pastures, while wild cherry trees bloomed alongside the road: a sign of hope and new beginnings. Her emotions swung from apprehension to excitement. Soon, she would see Dr. Westerly again. Or should she address him as Lord Westerly?

It was as though he were two men. Two sides of the same coin. It made him more complicated and infinitely more appealing since she did not know much about either man.

Nonsense. She was behaving like an infatuated goose. She most certainly was not anxious to see the man. Her eagerness stemmed from the prospect of doing something meaningful with her life while she waited for her child to be born.

Well, Lady Tinsworthy might believe that Elizabeth was exactly what her nephew needed, she presumed she referred to Elizabeth helping at the hospital and something more personal. Either way, Elizabeth had serious doubts. Her heart was closed to the possibility of love, and as for helping at the hospital, she had no training. What could she do that could help the doctor?

Her education had equipped her to excel at polite conversation about the weather, music, and the arts. A lady did not discuss politics or religion, as it was deemed beyond her capability to understand those topics. Elizabeth had read about the war between Britain and Napoleon, but a lady did not discuss such things either. Yet she knew that a majority of Dr. Westerly's hospital patients had received injuries in battle, and as a result, she was about to come face to face with the horrors she had been forbidden to discuss.

How would she react? Would she swoon, scream, or run from the room? Her reaction worried her more than the prospect of tending to the wounded. These men needed her care, not the confirmation that their injuries were life-threatening or hideous. She must find a way to cloak her reaction.

Lady Tinsworthy's suggestion that Dr. Westerly needed help running his hospital had spread through Glen Castle and became the primary topic of conversation, from the chimney sweeps and groomsmen to the footmen, maids, and cooks, and her ladyship's Ladies in Waiting. Everyone wanted to contribute. Many had offered to help when and where they could, and as a result a wagon loaded with food, clothing, and household essentials trailed behind the carriage.

It had been decided that because of the inclement weather conditions, those who wished to stay in Merwood could do so at Lady Tinsworthy's expense. Her ladyship also guaranteed that anyone wishing to stay on permanently at the hospital, and receiving Dr.

Westerly's agreement, could do so with her blessing and receive a generous salary.

Mrs. Neverly occupied the seat next to Elizabeth's. Miss Brown, her confinement ended, and insisting she be called Mary, dozed opposite them. Mary had declined the position as a servant to the village's vicar and his wife, preferring Dr. Westerly's hospital. She felt indebted to Dr. Westerly for helping her brother and wanted to show her gratitude. Miss Coalton felt it best to remain at Glen Castle as she was still not feeling well, but everyone knew she held out hope that her lover would have a change of heart and dash to Glen Castle with an offer of marriage and a special license.

For her part, Lady Tinsworthy vowed to drop by the hospital from time to time as soon as the new additions to her Ladies in Waiting—Miss Abernathy, Mrs. Kensington, and Miss Fairweather—were settled comfortably in their new quarters at Glen Castle.

Mrs. Neverly adjusted her bonnet's sky-blue ribbon, then leaned over toward the window on her side of the carriage. "The day is beautiful, is it not, Lady Montgomery?"

"We are friends," Elizabeth said. "Please call me Elizabeth. I am so tired of titles."

"Then you must call me Margerie," she said with a smile. "No one in polite society would believe we were friends. Me, the light o' love of a pirate and you a member of the *ton*."

Elizabeth had learned quite a bit about the lives of the Ladies in Waiting. Lady Tinsworthy created a warm and welcoming atmosphere where trust flourished. Elizabeth woke each morning grateful to Dr. Westerly for encouraging her to seek out Lady Tinsworthy.

Elizabeth settled back against the cushion, concentrating on the blur of color that sped by as the carriage rumbled over the countryside. No doubt the odd feeling she felt when she thought of Dr. Westerly was nothing more than gratitude.

Margerie sighed, a telltale sign that she was thinking of her pirate.

"Have you told him that you carry his child?" Elizabeth said.

"You knew I was thinking of the scoundrel—how very predictable of me. I cannot seem to purge him from my thoughts." Margerie continued to gaze out the window, resting her hand on her belly. "I never had the chance. I learned I carried his child only after he had set sail for the Americas. But it would not matter. Each time he returned, he vowed he loved me, pledged that he would not leave me again, and then he would receive word of hidden treasure or a newly discovered map and head out for parts unknown. I would rather raise this babe on my own than with a man who cares more for the sea than he does for those he professes to love."

Elizabeth reached over and gently squeezed Margerie's hand. "We are not that much alike, you and I. We face the prospect of raising our child alone. Except in your situation, the father of your child loves you. You should write to him."

"You always believe in a happily ever after," Margerie said sighing again. "Sage advice that you should follow yourself. You might not love the captain, nor he you, but he is the father of your child." Margerie patted Elizabeth's hand. "You must forgive yourself. You were grieving for your fiancé and vulnerable when you met the captain and fancied you had found love again, and you gave in to that dream. We all long for the miracle to love and be loved, do we not?"

"But I should have known better. I had known my fiancé for years. We were never intimate. We were the picture of propriety, and I turned his offer of marriage down a number of times before I accepted. Yet I knew the captain for only three or four weeks and believed every word he spoke. I was such a fool."

"You were not a fool," Margerie said, with a strong even voice. "You were human, and you must never forget you are not alone."

"Thank you, "Elizabeth said, hugging Margerie. The conversation always brought Elizabeth peace. As a child she had had few friends, but in a short span of time the Ladies in Waiting had all become very dear to her.

"But enough of our dwelling on the past," Margerie said. "It is the future we face. I, for one, am looking forward to working at Dr. Westerly's hospital. It is a welcome distraction from the tedium of waiting for our children to be born. Before I met my pirate, I managed my father's estate. Up until he lost our entire fortune in a game of cards, that is. Thank you for inviting me."

"I believe you insisted I take you with me."

Margerie nodded with a laugh. "That I did. I was so very bored I thought I would go mad. I never was one for needlework or quiet strolls in the garden, and I am a dreadful disaster on the pianoforte and cannot carry a tune in a bucket."

Mary jerked awake, losing her bonnet in the process. She yawned and bent to retrieve her bonnet. "'ave we arrived?"

"We have indeed, sleepyhead," Margerie said with a smile.

Merwood Hospital stood on the edge of town, a stately Georgian mansion, surrounded by well-kept grounds, with a fountain featuring the statue of Minerva in the center of the circular driveway. The estate marked the boundary between the lands of Glen Castle and those owned by Dr. Westerly's brother, the current Earl of Willowdown.

A young man—one with carrot red hair and dressed in a patched gray suit two sizes too large for him—rushed to meet the carriage. He set the steps in place and opened the carriage door.

"Name's Levie," he said, extending one hand as he held his faded top hat in place against the stiff wind. "I will have your luggage brought up to your rooms." He extended a scarred hand as he helped Elizabeth, Margerie, and Mary from the carriage.

"Thank you," Elizabeth said. "We will also need help unloading the supplies Lady Tinsworthy sent along with us. Is Dr. Westerly available?"

"He is in surgery, my lady," Levie said, as he looked beyond her toward the wagon loaded with food and goods. His eyes widened. "There are angels in this world. We are most grateful, my lady." Then he stepped aside as the wolfhound puppy raced to greet the carriage.

Elizabeth bent to rub the puppy behind his ear. "Hello, Finnegan," she said. "I have missed you." Finnegan woofed a happy greeting. The dog had grown well above the height of her waist. "Are you Dr. Westerly's butler?" she asked the young man.

He grinned, exposing a dimple on either side of his youthful face. "No, my lady, though I would be grateful for the opportunity, should his lordship deem me worthy. My father was a clergyman up north, but he and my mum died of consumption, so it was off to war for me. The doctor saved my life, you see, and I owes him. Said I was welcome here if I liked, and here is where I will stay, regardless of his brother's threats."

"You go on ahead, Elizabeth," Margerie said as she linked arms with Mary. "I know you are anxious to meet with Dr. Westerly. Please inform him that we will join him shortly. Mary and I will unpack, and I have a letter to write."

"Good for you." Elizabeth smiled. "I have high hopes your pirate will come for you. Perhaps on a glorious white steed."

Margerie laughed. "We will see. You believe in romance for everyone but yourself."

Chapter Eight

The entry of the Merwood Hospital looked as though it had been dipped in a bucket of white paint. Its whitewashed walls were devoid of portraits. The tile floors were the color of porcelain and the lone table in the center had been painted the same as the walls. Elizabeth shuddered. The entry looked as cold as ice.

Elizabeth's first inclination was to run, but she ducked her head to hide a smile. Her aversion to an all-white interior amused her. A few months ago, she might have viewed this place as elegant or fashionable.

When she first arrived at Glen Castle, her senses had been assaulted by what she had considered an excessive use of candles and the vulgar use of vibrant green, red, and gold Christmas colors. She had believed Lady Tinsworthy was a little mad to decorate with so much color and light. The estate where she grew up decorated its rooms in muted tones and used flowers sparingly. Until she spent time at Glen Castle, she never realized how gloomy and inhospitable her home had been in comparison.

With time, Elizabeth came to realize that her ladyship was a wise woman, and the year-round Christmas decorations had a purpose. Those who sought refuge at Glen Castle were in a fragile state. Her ladyship's Ladies in Waiting had been rejected by society or by those they loved. Christmas was an acknowledged joyous time of year, and by design she had recreated that warm and welcoming atmosphere.

"Lady Montgomery," Levie said with a bow, interrupting her thoughts. "His lordship has suggested that I offer you refreshments in the hospital's waiting room. Might I offer you tea? It will not take long to brew, and there are biscuits left from yesterday's breakfast."

"That is truly kind of you. Perhaps later."

He nodded slowly, as he closed the entry door behind her. On impulse she opened them again and, as she had hoped, Finnegan waited outside the door, wagging his tail expectantly. She stepped aside to allow him entry.

"Begging your pardon, my lady," Levie said, "but Finnegan is not allowed inside the hospital. Dr. Westerly said he causes too much mischief."

"Please do not worry. I will be sure to tell Dr. Westerly that it was all my idea." Her comment seemed to appease Levie as he motioned for her to follow him toward a spiral staircase to the second floor.

Elizabeth followed the would-be butler through a labyrinth of hallways, past drawing rooms that had been converted into dormitories. Empty single beds were lined up in rows, with fresh linens and blankets, a table positioned between each bed. The attention to cleanliness was commendable, but the absence of color was as chilling as her impression of the entry had been.

"Where are Dr. Westerly's patients?" she said.

"They are expected to arrive at the end of the week, my lady. God only knows how we will manage, though. Lady Montgomery, are you quite sure you wish to meet with Dr. Westerly in the infirmary? A lady of your delicate sensibilities should not be privy to the injuries men sustained at war. You might reconsider? His lordship did suggest that when you arrived, I should escort you to the hospital's waiting room for a spot of tea."

"Thank you, but that will not be necessary. I am anxious to meet with the doctor, and I assure you I am not as delicate as I appear."

She rested her hand on Finnegan's head. Levie, at the behest of Dr. Westerly, was doing everything in his power to dissuade her from viewing the injured patients, which only made her more determined.

Finnegan looked toward her with large, amber-colored eyes that reassured her that there was more to her than the ability to select fashionable clothes. She hoped he was correct.

Levie opened the double doors and bowed. "If you will excuse me, my lady, I should see to the luggage and supplies."

Before she could object, he had turned to retrace his steps along the long corridor.

Moans and a scream ruptured the silence in the hallway. Finnegan remained close by her side as she entered a world different from anything she had experienced. She had never visited a hospital, and the men she knew who had fought in Britan's war against Napoleon never spoke of their experiences. When she had asked, they changed the subject or said it was not a topic for a woman's tender ears. In retrospect, she had lived a very sheltered life.

A dozen beds lined the long narrow room, five of them occupied. The men's injuries were as varied as their ages. Some had bandaged head wounds, others had lost limbs or were badly scarred. Dr. Westerly stood changing the blood-soaked bandages of a patient on the far side of the room.

Elizabeth pressed her lips together to stifle a gasp at the sight of so much blood and pain. The last thing Dr. Westerly needed was to comfort a hysterical woman, so she willed herself to remain calm.

The doctor had lost weight in the weeks since she would last seen him, and there were dark circles under his eyes. It tugged at her heart. He took care of everyone. Who took care of him?

She had feared witnessing the condition of the patients would be her undoing, that she would retreat, never to return. The scene before her had the opposite effect. She wanted to stay and help. Even more than that, she wanted to help Dr. Westerly. He was very much like his aunt. They gave so much to others with little thought for themselves. She vowed that would change at least a little, very soon.

She reached down to pet Finnegan again. "Are you ready?" she whispered as she moved toward Dr. Westerly. Animals had a wonderful way of lifting spirits in even the most dire of circumstances. She hoped she was right in this.

The dog woofed, as though confirming that her assessment was correct. The dog's bark brought a smile to her lips, but a scowl to Dr. Westerly.

He closed his eyes briefly, rubbing them with the heel of his hand. "Dogs are not allowed in my hospital. What are you doing here?" he asked, with a tired edge to his voice. "And where is Levie? I gave him strict instructions that when you, Mrs. Neverly, and Miss Brown arrived, you all were to meet me in the hospital's waiting room."

"He did not say, but he went to help Mrs. Neverly and Miss Brown with their luggage. I am surprised there were no others to help him. Have you given them the day off?"

"Not quite." His voice sounded bitter. He crossed his arms over his chest. "Finnegan has been expressly forbidden inside the hospital."

Instead of his harsh words offending her, they strengthened her resolve. The dear man was almost asleep on his feet and looked as though he had not had a decent meal in who knew how long. What was more, she recognized his bluster. He thought by raging at her he could intimidate her into retreat. She was made of sterner stuff.

At that moment Finnegan trotted past them to nudge the hand of the man Dr. Westerly had been attending. The man's despondent expression brightened into a grin that spread over his face as he patted the dog on his head gently. Finnegan responded, wagging his tail, and the man chuckled, scratching the dog behind his ear.

Elizabeth smothered a smile. Finnegan had earned a special treat. She removed her coat, gloves, and hat and draped them over a vacant bed. "Finnegan and I are here to help," she said in a business tone. She wanted the doctor to take her seriously. She was here to help. "As I mentioned, Mrs. Neverly and Miss Brown are settling into their rooms and will join us momentarily. They are as anxious as I am to meet the other doctors and nurses."

"There is only me," he said evenly, closing the distance that separated them. "There is no one else."

She heard the hint of despair in his voice. How could one man in a hospital this size care for everyone? It was an impossible task. "How is that possible?" Her voice trailed off as she raised her gaze to meet his and gasped as he approached. She had forgotten how impossibly tall the man was.

"It is complicated," he said. Then he shrugged and laughed bitterly. "Actually, that is not true. It is quite simple. Other than Levie, no one will work for me. My brother has seen to it. He owns the town of Merwood." He shrugged again and turned to clean up the linens by the bedside table. "My problem, not yours, and under the circumstances, I will understand if you, Mrs. Neverly, and Miss Brown return to Glen Castle. When you leave, can you take Finnegan with you? I am sure he will be happier with my aunt."

The silence grew between them as Dr. Westerly continued to remove the blood-soaked linens. She felt a sense of overwhelming helplessness in the air. Although she might not know anything about how to run a hospital or care for the sick, she did know a thing or two about feeling helpless. Her fiancé had been murdered and no one had believed her at first when she said she suspected his cousin of murder. She had not given up then and she would not give up now. She had agreed to volunteer out of boredom. Now she had a purpose. This man needed her help.

She cleared her throat. "I cannot speak for Mrs. Neverly, or Miss Brown, but I will stay. And as for Finnegan, your patient's expression has improved since Finnegan's arrival. I have also observed that your patients are quite taken with him. The puppy is a welcome distraction from their injuries."

"Well said, milady," the young man petting Finnegan said. "I like your lady, Dr. Westerly. Will you introduce her to me?"

"I'd be wanting an introduction too," another man said.

"Me, as well," a soldier said, adjusting his eyepatch. "And Freddy, send Finnigan over to me before you rub all the fur off his head."

"She is not 'my lady,' " Dr. Westerly said. He shook his head. "Dash it all! Very well, may I introduce Lady Elizabeth Montgomery? She is not staying, and neither is Finnegan."

"Of course I am staying. I just told you I was." She turned to the patients and smiled, saying, "I am pleased to meet you all." And to Dr. Westerly, she informed, "As for Finnigan, you must reconsider. A dog will bring them enjoyment."

"My patients need rest, and Finnigan is still a puppy and very active."

"Beggin' your pardon," the man with the eyepatch said, "but all we do here is rest. A distraction would be welcome."

Elizabeth rested her hand on his arm. "Please reconsider. I will personally look after Finnigan. He will not be a bother. I promise. Besides, he has already lightened your patient's day." She was surprised at her boldness and slipped her hand from his arm. "I have overstepped. I apologize." What must the man think of her?

Dr. Westerly glanced at her for a moment, his forehead creasing in a frown. He then rubbed the back of his neck and glanced toward Finnegan and his patients and took a deep breath. "No need to apologize. You are correct. Finnegan does have a calming effect and we are sorely in need of little cheer."

"And a woman's touch," Freddy shouted. His

comment was met with a round of applause. "No offense, Doc, but you're not that pretty to look at."

Dr. Westerly's mouth edged up at the corners. "No offense taken. Lady Montogomery and Finnigan can stay for a few days."

She watched as Dr. Westerly joked good naturally with the men. His demeanor had softened, and his eyes crinkled at the corners when he smiled. Freddy was wrong. Dr. Westerly was exceedingly pretty to look at. Well, perhaps 'pretty' was not the right word. But the word goodlooking did not capture him either. He was a man who could command a room.

She laced her hands in front of her. She had secured Finnigan's place here. The next step was to show that she could be of value as well. She did not have training as a nurse, and until she did, she wanted to make sure she was useful.

"Dr. Westly," she said, gaining his attention. "I will do whatever is needed here. I am not afraid of demanding work. But I can also read to the men while you do your rounds. The only book I have brought with me is Jane Austen's *Emma*. Does Merwood have a bookstore?"

He combed his hand through his hair. "You are with child, as are the other ladies who have invaded the hospital. Arduous work is out of the question. I will not have you all jeopardizing the health of the babes you carry. But you are all welcome to read to the men. I am not sure about the bookstore."

"No matter," she said pulling up a chair in the center of the room. "I will begin reading the novel I brought from Glen Castle."

"You intend to stay here?"

"Of course. Was there any doubt?"

His eyes crinkled at the corners again as he shook his head slowly. "I have been abominably rude to you, and for that I apologize. Yet you persisted. You are unlike any woman I have ever met. Even my aunt would not have defied me in this manner."

"I will take that as a compliment, my lord."

Chapter Nine

The next morning, the miserly rays of the morning sun were as weak as Elizabeth's tea as she sat opposite Margerie in the hospital's small waiting room that also served as the dining room. Even the fire in the hearth struggled to put out any heat. There was not a vase of flowers or a colorful pillow anywhere in sight, and the tables and chairs were scattered around the room in a haphazard fashion. It was a thoroughly depressing room.

"We should return to the infirmary," she said to Margerie, stifling a yawn. She was worried about Dr. Westerly. He could not continue at this pace, stealing snippets of sleep where he could and barely eating enough to sustain a small bird.

When Margerie and Mary had joined her last night, they had helped Dr. Westerly make his patients comfortable for the evening, but he had been adamant that he would not leave the infirmary to sleep or eat. Food she could bring to him, and she understood why he refused to leave the infirmary, so she made up a cot for him.

Margerie pushed her tea aside and pulled a face. "This tea tastes like it was brewed with used tea leaves and floor sweepings. What I would not give for a good cup of tea. I should have offered Levie my help unloading the supply wagon last night. I am sure we packed tea. I doubt Lady Tinsworthy is aware of the sorry situation."

"She would be appalled," Elizabeth said, "and attempt to hire more servants, which would only result in the same outcome. According to Dr. Westerly, his brother has the town of Merwood under his control and gave express orders that no one was allowed to work here. We can help, of course, but the hospital needs doctors and nurses—and more than just the three of us as helpers—to keep it running. Where is Mary? I am worried about her. She gave birth only a fleeting time ago and needs her rest."

"Mary assured me she is fit as a fiddle. She tasted the tea and stale biscuits and headed straight for the kitchen, and by the clatter of pots and pans I heard thirty minutes ago, she has taken control of what she considers heaven. She worked in the kitchens of a big estate before…well, before the lord of the manor fired her when he learned his son had impregnated her. If you ask me, she plans to take over as Dr. Westerly's cook and will be incredibly happy to do so."

"This gives me an idea," Elizabeth said. "What do you think of our asking Lady Tinsworthy if she thinks her Ladies in Waiting would be interested in working at Dr. Westerly's hospital two or three hours each day? Her ladyship also employs doctors and nurses, who are loyal only to her."

"Brilliant, and I noticed you were reading to the men last night. As much as I love the romance of a good Jane Austen novel, I believe the men would like more variety. Something along the order of Jonathan Swift's *Gulliver's Travels* or Daniel Defoe's *Robinson Crusoe* or Henry Fielding's *Tom Jones*. We could order them from that huge bookstore in London. How soon should we contact Lady Tinsworthy?"

"There is no time like the present. I will write a letter for Levie to take to her this morning. Meanwhile, you and I will return to help Dr. Westerly with his patients."

****

Thomas woke with a start from the cot in the infirmary. The last thing he remembered was serving his patients weak chicken broth for lunch, then sitting down to rest. He must have fallen asleep. The position of the sun outside the window suggested late afternoon. His patients were his first concern. The second was the noise. The infirmary buzzed with activity, like a beehive in the height of summer.

"What are all these people doing here?" he stormed, rising to his feet.

A gentleman in a dark suit was bent over, taking the pulse of a patient with an arm in a sling. A woman in a nurse's uniform fluffed the pillows of the man with the eye patch, while another woman whom he recognized as Mrs. Neverly sat reading aloud to the remaining patients, who gazed at her in rapt attention.

Lady Montgomery materialized as though from thin air and placed her hand on his arm, gazing up at him with those remarkable eyes of hers. "We are here to help."

Her touch both unsettled and calmed him. Where had she come from? "Lady Montgomery…"

"Please call me Lady Elizabeth," she said in that voice that reminded him of a spring breeze. "Before you list your objections, let me explain. This morning, I contacted your aunt and described your challenge."

"Challenge?" he said cocking an eyebrow. "People refusing to work for me is more than a challenge."

Lady Elizabeth pressed her full lips together to stifle

a smile, a habit he was beginning to recognize, although why she would want to hide her smile baffled him. She was even more lovely when she smiled.

"Yes, well…" she said, "your aunt may have solved that issue, whatever we wish to call it. Your brother might control the people in Merwood, but those who work for Lady Tinsworthy are loyal to her alone. Come, I want to introduce you to Dr. Wilkes and Mrs. Carlise. Your aunt has asked her Ladies in Waiting if they would like to help, as well."

"You are awake," a woman Thomas recognized as Miss Brown said as she approached. "Lady Elizabeth gave us orders that you were not to be disturbed unless the hospital was on fire or under attack." Miss Brown set a tray on the table beside his cot and lifted the dome lid off a plate.

"Is that a toasted cheese?" he said, his stomach grumbling in appreciation.

"Indeed." She beamed. "Made with cheddar and anchovies on ciabatta bread. Lady Tinsworthy mentioned that it was your favorite as a child. There is also tea and my specialty—a cinnamon-and-apple tart. With your approval, my lord, I am applying for the position of your new cook."

He glanced toward the cold broth beside the tray Miss Brown had set on the table. Levie had done what he could, but the lad was not a cook. The most that could be said was that Levie's soup was fresher and more nutritious than the meals Thomas had eaten when he was in the military.

He made a short bow toward Miss Brown. "I know I speak for my patients as well as myself when I say that we would be forever grateful to you, Miss Brown. I fear

Levie, although possessing many talents, would be the first to admit he has little skill when it comes to cooking. I would be honored if you would agree to be the hospital's head cook."

Miss Brown bobbed her thank you and looked for a moment as though she might hug Thomas. Instead, she bobbed another curtsy and cleared away the cold soup.

Thomas took in the orderly and respectful way Dr. Wilkes and his nurse addressed Thomas's patients as they asked them questions. Last night Thomas had feared he would have to close the hospital. Lady Elizabeth had been correct. A hospital needed more than one doctor.

"Lady Elizabeth, might I have a word in private?"

He chose a quiet alcove near a window that overlooked the rolling hills where sheep grazed contentedly in the afternoon sun. Lady Elizabeth had changed her clothes since he had last seen her. Her dress was a shade of pink with meadow green trim that reminded him of tulips and the first blush of spring.

He had no right to feel an attraction toward her. She carried another man's child and he assumed that meant that she felt an affection for the man, even though her doctor in London said the cad had abandoned her. But surely the man would come to his senses. Lady Elizabeth was remarkable.

"You wanted to talk with me, Dr. Westerly?"

"I wish to thank you. You have saved the hospital."

"You give me too much credit, my lord. Lady Tinsworthy has the resources. I merely made a few suggestions."

"Beautiful and humble."

Her face flushed the shade of her dress. "My lord…"

He clasped his hands behind his back. "I apologize.

That was uncalled for. Please accept my apology."

Her lips curled slightly at the corner. "There was something I wished to ask you."

"Anything."

She hesitated, averting her gaze from his. "Might I decorate the hospital? It is so gloomy. I particularly admire the way Lady Tinsworthy decorates Glen Castle as though it were Christmas year-round. What do you think?"

Thomas thought that if she had asked him to paint the walls purple with red and black polka dots, he would have gone out and purchased paintbrushes.

Chapter Ten

Months rolled by, gaining momentum as they raced into late October. Once again, the nights were dark and laced with frost, but Elizabeth did not mind. The days smelled crisp and clean and, like today, were filled with sunshine. She settled on the stone bench by the hospital's garden to catch her breath. In their spare time, she and Margerie had helped bring order back to the hedges, rose bushes, and ornamental trees. At first, Dr. Westerly had not understood the importance of restoring the flower beds and meandering paths to their former glory.

She tucked a letter into the pocket of her dress and bent down to cup one of the last remaining black-eyed susans in the palm of her hand, smiling when she remembered the doctor's cocked eyebrow when she told him that the reason she wanted to restore the gardens was that she believed nature had healing powers.

His blank stare convinced her she should amend her argument. She suggested the gardens would offer his recovering patients a welcome change from walking the hospital's hallways for exercise. Her tactic had worked, and the gardens became a welcome retreat for both patients and other occupants of the hospital.

The garden lay dormant now, but in the spring, it would burst into color again.

Elizabeth closed her eyes, tilting her head to bask in the soft fall sunlight filtering through the trees. She had been more tired than usual these past few weeks. Lady Tinsworthy said it was because her time of lying-in was near and suggested she should consider leaving for Glen Castle where they were more suited to help her with the birth of her child. Elizabeth had dismissed the concern. Lady Tinsworthy worried overmuch. Elizabeth informed her ladyship that her baby was not due for at least several weeks.

Elizabeth heard the rustle of skirts and looked up and smiled. "Margerie, I thought you were on your way to Glen Castle for your lying-in?"

Margerie rubbed her belly in a wide circle. "Not yet. My carriage awaits, and I am here to convince you to come with me. Lady Tinsworthy is genuinely concerned."

"She need not be. My doctor in London assured me that the babe is due toward the first of November at the earliest. I have plenty of time. Besides, I need to stay here and help Dr. Westerly."

"As you are aware, Dr. Westerly has more than enough help, thanks to you and Lady Tinsworthy. Glen Castle's monthly nurse suggested her sister, Mrs. Potter, is a nurse and looking for a position for both her and her daughter. They are working out splendidly, and so is Dr. Wilkes. Mr. Wentworth, the accoucheur at Glen Castle, recommended him."

"All wonderful staff additions here," Elizabeth said. "Dr. Wilkes and Dr. Westerly studied together and have become great friends."

Margerie eased down on the bench and sighed deeply. "Oh, but this babe likes to kick. I swear, if his pirate father ever does show up, I am going to give the man a piece of my mind for putting me through this. It is a wonder that women ever have a second child, after going through it once."

"They say we forget the pain and discomfort we experienced in childbirth."

"Pish. Dosh. That sounds like something a man made up."

Elizabeth smiled. "It does indeed. I am going to miss you."

Margerie smoothed the folds of her dress over her belly. "I am not going far. I have decided to stay at Glen Castle after my child is born." She hesitated. "I received a letter from Miss Coalton, or should I say, Mrs. Woolcut. She and her new husband arrived in Devonshire last week and are happily anticipating the birth of the babe."

Elizabeth patted the letter she had secured in her pocket. "Lady Tinsworthy does have a matchmaker's gift. She introduced Miss Coalton and Mr. Woolcut at one of her balls. I should not have been so stubborn. Her ladyship does have a knack for knowing if two people belong together. I am about to become an unwed mother, yet I refused to ask Lady Tinsworthy for help in finding a husband."

"We are both stubborn. I am waiting for my pirate, and you are holding out hope that your captain will answer your letter."

Elizabeth produced the letter from her pocket and showed it to her friend. "It was returned unopened."

"I'm so sorry."

"I do not know what I expected. A miracle or a knight in shining armor." She traced the name of the captain on the letter. "I was not completely truthful. When I realized I was carrying his child, I went to look for him. I did not find him, but his commanding officer told me that he already had a wife." She returned the letter to her pocket. "I wrote him because I thought he at least needed to know he was father to a child here."

Margerie squeezed Elizabeth's hand. "Please reconsider and come with me. You look so tired. Lady Tinsworthy is not the only one who is worried about you."

Elizabeth pushed to her feet. "Come. You have a long journey to Glen Castle. I will walk you to the carriage. Do not worry. Inform Lady Tinsworthy that I promise I will plan to come next week."

Chapter Eleven

A few days later, laughter drew Thomas's attention toward the far side of the infirmary as he did his rounds. Lady Elizabeth was reading to a young man who had survived a broken and lacerated arm after falling from a tree. The incident reminded Thomas of the first time he had seen Lady Elizabeth. She had been climbing a tree to save a stranded kitten, unmindful of the spectacle she had caused. Her tendency to rescue those in need extended to every living thing. A trait he highly admired.

Her raven hair was pulled into a loose knot at the base of her neck, and the soothing tones of her voice as she read aloud carried over the groan of creaking floorboards and the business of running an infirmary. Her voice was music to his ears.

Over the course of the last several months, his hospital not only had been transformed but had thrived under Lady Elizabeth's nurturing care. Miss Brown proved to be an exemplary cook and Mrs. Neverly managed the household as diligently as though it were her own. As for Lady Elizabeth, he could not imagine his life without her in it. She was the hospital's very heart and soul.

Lady Elizabeth was in the advanced stages of her pregnancy but looked as elegant as ever. She wore a high-waisted, long-sleeved, emerald-green dress, with lace trim at the neck and bodice. His aunt's seamstress had expertly redesigned the gown to flow over Lady Elizabeth's rounded belly. She was lovely, and dressed impeccably, but it was her smile, and her voice when she read to the patients that he looked forward to every day.

He considered Lady Elizabeth a breath of spring. True to her promise, she had covered every doorway, archway, and banister of the hospital with Christmas-themed finery that rivaled Glen Castle's decorations.

But she was an unwed mother, and he knew that must weigh heavily on her shoulders, yet she never spoke of her delicate predicament.

He knew firsthand the consequences of a child born out of wedlock. In his case, he did not know why his mother, or father, left him on the orphanage front step, but he could conjecture.

His mother was a courtesan, and the child was inconvenient. His father might have been a member of the nobility and impregnated one of his servants. Every child in the orphanage romanticized their parents' reasons for abandoning them. Some even believed their fathers or mothers, or both, were royalty.

The likely scenario was that their parents were as poor as church mice and could not afford another mouth to feed. When he was a child, he blamed his parents for his predicament. Time and experience had taught him that the world was not constructed with easy answers and easy solutions, regardless of one's status in life, particularly if you had been dealt an unfavorable hand. It had been a long journey, but he had learned to forgive his parents. God knows he had made his own mistakes.

He would have liked to add that the bullying and name-calling had stopped, but it had not, and regardless of Lady Elizabeth's money and position, the shadow of her as an unwed mother would fall heaviest on her child.

Dr. Wilkes joined him on his rounds. "A quiet night. I talked with Mrs. Potter and her daughter and told them they could retire for the evening. I am having second thoughts, however. Lady Elizabeth looks as though she might go into labor at any moment. It was unfortunate that she did not accompany Mrs. Neverly to Glen Castle last week."

Thomas had been so preoccupied with caring for his patients he had neglected to note the signs. The paleness of her skin, the evenly timed moments when she pressed her lips together as though she were in pain now registered—and her extended belly looked as though it had dropped lower. Wilkes was correct. Lady Elizabeth was in labor. He would summon a carriage and have her taken to Glen Castle at once. His aunt had a permanent suite of lying-in chambers prepared for her Ladies in Waiting, as well as a capable staff of doctors and nurses.

Thomas concentrated on Lady Elizabeth's voice again with more care as she read to the young man with the broken arm. She had elected to read *Tom Jones*, by Henry Fielding. It was a lively tale of adventure and a story of Tom's enduring love for Sophia. But the tone of Lady Elizabeth's voice was strained as she read, and her facial features pinched as though she fought to hide that she was experiencing labor pains.

"Wilkes, you may be right regarding Lady Elizabeth going into labor," Thomas said, revising his assessment to order a carriage. "At this late hour, the winding, coastal roads to Glen Castle are not easy to navigate under the best of conditions. But late at night, with rain, the roads are treacherous. A carriage wheel could hit a rut in the road and split apart, leaving her stranded. A horse could twist his leg or throw a shoe. The dangers are endless. I could accompany her, of course, but that would be reckless. She must stay here. Please ask Mrs. Potter and her daughter to stay a little longer and prepare a bed for Lady Elizabeth. I will check on the lady. I need to convince her to lie down."

"She will tell you she does not need to rest."

"No doubt."

He schooled his expression to remain calm as he joined her beside the young man's bedside. He had learned as an officer in the military that if he exuded confidence and calm to those under his command, his men believed success was possible. A calm and confident demeanor was equally true for a doctor. If he appeared concerned, the patient might panic.

"Lady Elizabeth, might I have a word?"

She had paused in her reading to press her hand against her lower back. Her eyes pressed closed as the book slipped from her grasp.

Thomas caught her in his arms before she fell. Her back arched as a spasm tore through her body. Her contractions were advanced. Without complications, the babe would be arriving within the next few hours. How she had managed to stay calm was a miracle.

"Wilkes! Mrs. Potter!" Thomas shouted. "We need that bed. Now!"

With Lady Elizabeth in his arms, Thomas headed toward where Mrs. Potter prepared a bed on the far side of the infirmary. Lady Elizabeth had slumped against him, her face turned away. Her eyes were shut as tears cut a path down her cheeks.

"I am unwed," she said with a sob. "My father and brother will be ruined and never speak to me again, and what will happen to my child?"

Thomas traversed the infirmary, holding her closer against his chest. She faced impossible odds and everything she said was true. The scandal would touch every member of her family. She rarely spoke of her brother other than to say that he was single and living on the Continent. After the scandal broke, his prospect of finding a suitable wife might prove difficult. But Lady Elizabeth had not mentioned how these circumstances reflected on her. True to her character, she had thought only of how it would affect others.

"Lady Montgomery. I will marry ye," a patient said as Thomas passed beside the young man, who held his crutch in the air.

"Save your breath, Harry," a baldheaded man nursing an injured hand said. "'Tis me she fancies. Ain't that right, Lady Montgomery?"

Mrs. Potter and Dr. Wilkes set about to quiet the men and assure them that Lady Montgomery appreciated their offers of marriage, but it was out of the question. Lady Montgomery had a child to birth, and her focus was on her babe, not matrimony.

Lady Elizabeth's eyes were hooded as Thomas placed her on the bed and drew a blanket over her belly. Her gaze was averted as though she was staring into a void. "I should marry one of the men who offered to marry me." Her voice sounded as though she were speaking more to herself than to him.

The men quieted as Mrs. Potter, a woman as round as a teapot and with a smile for everyone she met, hurried to stand at the foot of Lady Elizabeth's bed. Mrs. Potter was a widow. Her son, Reginald, had also survived war wounds, and in gratitude, she had vowed to help others in the same way her son had been helped.

"Begging your pardon, Doctor," Mrs. Potter said with a hint of the retired schoolteacher in her tone, "but her ladyship cannot stay here with all these men while she births her child. I did my best to place her as far away as possible, but she needs her privacy."

Thomas looked about him. "Devil take it," he swore under his breath, realizing with sudden shock that Mrs. Potter was correct. His patients might have quieted down, but every one of them was focused on Lady Elizabeth. He should have seen it himself. She would need a private room. "Thank you, of course you are right. There is a suite of rooms on the top floor that my aunt uses when she visits. We will move Lady Elizabeth there at once."

She had closed her eyes again and whispered a "Thank you." Mentioning she should marry one of the soldiers making her an offer in the infirmary highlighted how desperate she had felt. Her child would be born a bastard.

Because of Lady Elizabeth's wealth and status, no one would daresay a disparaging word in her or her child's presence. But the cut direct would be more subtle and, in many ways, more hurtful, as it would be unexpected and catch her off guard. Excuses would be made why she was excluded from events. But her suffering would pale compared to that of her child's. The taunts and fights had not stopped after Thomas had been adopted by the Earl of Willowdown. If anything, they had become more vicious. It was not a life he would wish on anyone.

A dreadful roar of shouts, overlaid with commands to make way, split the air. His aunt's cherry-red traveling clothes had a military cut to them, sporting brass buttons and ornamental shoulder epaulettes. Like the point of a spear, Lady Tinsworthy marched into the infirmary ahead of an entourage of an assortment of five somber-faced men and women. One he recognized as the Vicar Chesterfield.

His aunt held a staying hand. "I must see Lady Elizabeth."

"Aunt, we have things well in hand."

"Clearly, you do not," she said, as she reached for Lady Elizabeth's hand. "Dear child, your hand is as cold as ice. Margerie told me that she believed you were close to going into labor. I came as quickly as I could to make the arrangements. Due to the urgency, I had to call in several favors. I would have wished that you were at Glen Castle, but we will make do. As it turns out, Margerie also went into labor, so Mr. Wentworth and Mrs. Morris are with Margerie, but I have faith in my nephew, along with Dr. Wilkes and Mrs. Potter."

"As do I," Lady Elizabeth managed to say, but the hand she held over her belly clenched. Good Lord, the lady was in labor and still managed to remain poised.

"Why haven't you taken Elizabeth to my suites?" his aunt said. "You must do so at once."

Her clipped order took Thomas by surprise. It was not like his aunt to question his authority in matters that concerned his patients. He could only attribute this break in protocol as stemming from her concern for Lady Elizabeth. Well, he was concerned as well.

"We were preparing to do so when you arrived," he said gently. "Although I am grateful for your concern, as you have observed, Lady Elizabeth is in labor, and I promise you that I will not leave her side. Kindly ask these people to wait downstairs. Their presence disrupts our ability to care for our patients."

Lady Tinsworthy did not budge but folded her arms over her waist instead. "These people will remain as they were. They are here for a reason. May I introduce Merwood's Vicar Chesterfield and his wife, Mrs. Sarah Chesterfield. I have procured a special license, the vicar is here to perform the wedding ceremony, and his wife has graciously consented to function as the witness. All is as it should be. I have run out of patience with you and Lady Elizabeth. Thankfully, I am here to set matters right. You and Elizabeth are to be married before her child is born."

The infirmary plunged into silence as all its occupants focused on Lady Elizabeth. She stiffened noticeably. "God's teeth!" she said. "I am not marrying anyone."

Her outburst stunned his aunt into silence as Thomas hid a smile. Even in the throes of labor pain she refused to allow anyone to bully her into doing something she did not want to do.

His admiration for her grew. But his aunt had proposed an intriguing solution. If Lady Elizbeth had been amenable to the offer, would he agree to the match?

Chapter Twelve

The patients in the infirmary burst into conversation, shattering the silence. Everyone voiced their opinion. Voices grew louder until they blended in a cacophony of sound. Elizabeth traced a wide circle over her belly with her hand, uneasy at the undue attention. In the corner, Lady Tinsworthy and Dr. Westerly were engaged in a heated discussion. Nearby, the vicar, his wife, and their entourage looked equally as concerned.

Everyone wanted to determine her fate. No one bothered to ask what she wanted. But what *did* she want?

Elizabeth draped her arm over her eyes to prevent them from giving in to rebellious tears.

How absurd.

She never cried.

She blamed the full moon outside the window by her bed. It was too bright.

Over the last month, bright moon or dull, overcast day, she had been a veritable watering pot. And now Lady Tinsworthy suggested she wed Dr. Westerly. He had looked as bewildered as she had felt. Of course he had not wanted to marry her. She carried another man's child. Why had his aunt made such an outrageous suggestion?

Before her world had been turned upside down, Dr. Westerly would have been considered a suitable match. He was intelligent, kind, titled, the sole heir to his aunt's large estate, and dangerously handsome. Was she mad for refusing the offer?

The babe kicked as the beginning of another labor pain shuddered to life. They were coming closer and closer together. This would not do. She was not prepared to be a mother. She drew her mouth together in a thin line and draped her free arm on top of the other.

She had been fortunate as a child. Her father believed in education for both his children and that his daughter should have the same tutors as his son. She lived surrounded by lovely things and her life seemed the stuff of fairy tales. It was expected that she would marry well, give birth to beautiful children, and become an important member of the *ton*. Then her fiancé had been murdered and she witnessed the seamy side of life.

Her girlhood dream was that when she announced she was with child, the father would be overjoyed, and they would share their happiness with their friends and family. After their child was born, there would be a christening and parties to celebrate the happy event. Her life attending the theater, going for promenades and carriage rides in Hyde Park, and enjoying ices at Gunter's would resume. London was the center of the universe and there would be opportunities for stimulating conversations. She would seek to work for the Crown again. Those dreams were no longer possible. As an unwed mother, she would be ostracized by the very society from whom she sought approval.

She had believed that over time she would grow accustomed to the quiet life of the country, believing it an ideal solution away from those who would judge her and her child harshly. She had been living in a dream world. She missed London. Even as the child within her grew, she had somehow thought this day would never come.

A man cleared his throat. "How are we doing?"

She recognized Dr. Westerly's voice and his calm demeanor grated on her nerves. "We? Do you feel as though your back will break every time you have a labor pain?"

He offered a small bow, and she noted the twinkle in his eye. "My apologies, Lady Elizabeth. How are *you* doing?"

She swiped at her eyes, then settled her arms over her belly. "My labor pains have slowed."

"They have not," he said, glancing over the clipboard he held. She did not know what made her angrier, that he had disregarded her assessment or that there was a document on her condition on a clipboard. He was treating her like an ordinary patient.

"Did you hear me?" she said.

"Humm."

Mrs. Potter appeared and whispered to him that Lady Elizabeth's accommodations were ready.

Dr. Westerly nodded, setting the clipboard on the hook attached to the railing of Elizabeth's bed before he spoke. "As I am sure you are aware, in your condition it is unacceptable for you to stay in the infirmary with the men. You need private quarters."

His stoic demeanor pressed around her throat. She swallowed. He was right, of course, but he had used his formal voice, the one he used when he believed the patient would not cooperate. But of course, that was exactly how she had behaved—like a difficult patient. The doctor was trying to help, and she was argumentative. The realization made her feel alone and helpless at a time when she needed people the most. This situation was all her fault. Despite her protests to the country, her baby would be born, and she could not do this on her own.

"Thank you," she said. "Privacy is appreciated. I did not mean to cause so much trouble." She gave a slight nod, holding back a flood of melancholy and despair. She had made such a cake of herself. How unbearable foolish she had been. One night with a man she barely knew, one people had warned her to shun, had changed her life forever.

Dr. Westerly's hazel eyes deepened to a dark green. She understood that expression. She had witnessed it numerous times when he attended his patients. He was trying to understand her pain. "It is no trouble, Lady Elizabeth. I have…I have had much on my mind and am at fault, not you. I should have recognized your distress earlier. It is I who owe you an apology. With your permission," he said, his voice lowered only for her to hear, "I will carry you to your new quarters. If you would prefer someone else…"

"No, you will do." She bit her lip, realizing how that might have sounded. "I am sorry. I am doing it again. That was uncalled for and rude. Forgive me. I am not myself. I sound ungrateful for your help, and I assure you that I am not. I am usually the one in control, you see."

There was a flash of tenderness in his eyes. "I understand, more than you might realize," he said as he gathered her in his arms as though she were as light as the feather pillow on her bed.

"Lady Tinsworthy suggesting that we wed was inappropriate," she said, after clearing her throat. It was not just the loss of control that concerned her. It was the unexplainable vulnerability she felt whenever she was near the doctor. "I am sure you were insulted by her interference."

"Was I?" he said as he traversed the infirmary toward the exit. She felt the muscles of his chest flex as though he were suppressing a chuckle. "You are an extraordinary and formidable woman, you know. You put my aunt in her place when you refused her suggestion that we marry. I have never seen her at a loss of words."

"Poppycock. I am an ordinary woman."

"Humm. We shall agree to disagree, Lady Elizabeth," he said as he left the infirmary and ascended the stairs to the top floor. "But perhaps my aunt's offer is not as mad as it seems."

Chapter Thirteen

The doctor's words rang in Elizabeth's ears as he ducked his head entering Lady Tinsworthy's suite of rooms. *But perhaps my aunt's offer is not as mad as it seems.*

But she could not marry Dr. Westerly. The mere suggestion seemed preposterous. Marrying the doctor would mean the end of her dream to marry for love. She respected him tremendously. He was a good man, of that she had no doubt, and honorable, and a bleeding heart to those in need. He had never turned a patient away, regardless of their ability to pay. He had climbed a tree because he thought she meant to jump from it and end her life. But was respect enough for a good marriage?

Mrs. Potter had hurried ahead of Elizabeth and was bent over a four-poster bed as she fluffed pillows and smoothed back a cream-colored quilt embroidered with tiny pink and yellow rosebuds.

The room had a cheery, happy feel that should have lifted Elizabeth's spirits. Instead, her mood plummeted. The room reminded her of her bedroom when she had been a child. The walls were covered with scenes of meadows teeming with wildflowers and children dancing round a May Pole. A bank of windows, covered with draperies the same pattern as the quilt, was on the river side of the room, with a writing desk and wardrobe on the other.

Dr. Westerly laid her on the four-poster bed and stepped back. "What a lovely bed, Lady Elizabeth. And the draperies are your favorite color, rose pink, I believe."

Why did he think she liked pink?

"I detest pink," Elizabeth said, knowing she was acting like a petulant child as she glanced toward Dr. Westerly before turning again toward Mrs. Potter. "This is nonsense. It is the middle of October. I have been informed that my child will not arrive until the first week in November. Our family physician assured me, when I first learned I was with child, that I would deliver this babe on November tenth." She knew she was rambling, but it helped her keep her mind off what she now considered a desperate situation. "So, as you can see, I have plenty of time before the birth. Dr. Merryweather said the positioning and shape of my pelvis indicates that I will have an easy birth, no more than one or two hours of labor at most. I do believe the pains have subsided, which makes you wrong, Dr. Westerly," she said with a sidelong glance toward him.

She took a breath, pressing her hand on her side, and blinking as pain rolled over her in a wave. It felt as though her backbone was fracturing.

"A fine set of rooms," Dr. Wilkes said, entering the room. His voice boomed cheerfully, his wide smile highlighting the gleam of white teeth and an overbite. "Are we all comfortably settled?"

"Do all doctors talk to patients using the royal *we*?" Elizabeth said, glowering first at Dr. Wilkes, then toward Dr. Westerly.

"It is the first lesson learned at university," Dr. Westerly said in his calm voice. She knew his tone was intended to soothe her rattled nerves, but it had the opposite effect. She wanted to rail and shout and shake her fist.

She turned her wrath toward him. "I am not having this child today!"

"Well, there you have it," Dr. Wilkes said, his smile firmly in place. "Women know more about these things than the mere mortal male, or so my sister keeps reminding me."

Elizabeth threw a pillow in Dr. Wilkes' direction. Dr. Westerly caught it in his grasp before it hit its mark. "Wilkes, I think it best that you take your leave. The Lady Elizabeth does not appreciate your sense of humor and we are not needed. She has been informed that her child will arrive in November."

"Indeed," Wilkes said, his eyebrow rising. "November, you say? Extraordinary. A saying *when pigs fly* comes to mind."

"I could not have phrased it better myself," Dr. Westerly said.

"I believe I will stand at a safe distance, away from flying pillows, however." Dr. Wilkes said. "Lady Elizabeth, I wish you well." Wilkes bowed slightly and moved to converse with Mrs. Potter who was folding linen towels, to prepare for the birth of Elizabeth's child.

Dr. Westerly paused for a few heartbeats, then crossed to place the pillow behind Elizabeth's head. "You are in labor, despite what Dr. Merryweather claimed. The babe is not waiting until November."

"I will have you know that Dr. Merryweather is a highly respected surgeon in London. He oversaw not only my birth and my brother's, but a vast number of the births of members of the *ton*. You are wrong. This babe will arrive in November."

"I respect Dr. Merryweather. He was one of my mentors, but I most assuredly am not wrong on the timing of the birth of your child. It is imminent."

Elizabeth folded her arms over her belly. "This bed is too soft. I liked the bed in the infirmary better. I prefer to sit, or better yet, leave." Elizabeth tried to pull herself to a sitting position and failed, then batted Dr. Westerly's hands away. "And I overheard what you said to Dr. Wilkes. *When pigs fly.* What an utterly absurd expression."

Dr. Westerly helped her straighten against the pillows and pulled the blanket over her stomach. "You were meant to overhear my comment, madam. Perhaps Dr. Merryweather's prediction of the timing of your birth was accurate. But there are many factors that can alter such a prediction. My biggest concern with Dr. Merryweather is that he should have informed you of the variables. He could not predict with complete accuracy how you would fare with the birth of your first child."

"Perhaps he did not want to frighten me," she said. "My mother almost died when I was born."

Dr. Westerly winced, then recovered to lift his chin. "I am sorry to hear that your mother experienced a difficult birth. I hope she recovered and is well."

Elizabeth turned her head to gaze in the direction of the window, blinking as she bit down gently on her lower lip before saying, "My mother died giving birth to my brother."

He paused, his expression in shadows. "I am truly sorry. This is your first child and you have informed me that your mother died in childbirth. Dr. Merryweather should have taken these factors into consideration and advised you to begin your lying-in sooner."

"Has anyone ever told you that you have a terrible bedside manner?"

"A time or two," he said with a slight curve of his mouth.

Elizabeth glanced around the annoyingly wide shoulders of Dr. Westerly and raised her voice to address Dr. Wilkes. "Is Dr. Westerly always this blunt? I do not like his manner. Aren't doctors required to give comfort to their patients?" She straightened to glare at Dr. Westerly, biting down on her lip again as she felt another labor pain. She would not give the man the satisfaction of knowing the pains were coming closer and closer together. But she had the annoying feeling he already knew.

"Well, Dr. Westerly," Dr. Wilkes said, "you have been firmly put in your place. I have been saying for years that your bedside manner needs softening, and now you have heard a patient complaining of it, or the lack thereof, that is."

"Go to blazes, Wilkes." Dr. Westerly said as he gave Elizabeth a slight bow. "If you are determined to have this babe wait until November tenth for his coming out, as it were, I advise you to stay as calm as you can. I have witnessed that when the mother is prone to irritability and over-excitement, the child will respond in kind."

"That is absurd," Elizabeth said. "I am never irritable, and I am always calm. You are saying that to annoy me. You are the reason for my unsettled mood." Elizabeth grimaced and pressed her hand down on the side of her stomach. "I think my babe just kicked me."

Dr. Westerly bowed again. "Smart lad or lassie. I will be nearby and will instruct Mrs. Potter to contact me when your labor pains grow more frequent. A few moments without us hovering around might indeed calm your nerves. I will be outside having a coffee with Wilkes."

"You can go to hell, for all I care."

"Your wish is my command, my lady, but I will be close at hand, nonetheless." He ducked as a pillow flew past his head.

Chapter Fourteen

With a bow, Thomas heeded Lady Elizabeth's order to leave her rooms, on the way giving Mrs. Potter instructions to provide Lady Montgomery with pen and paper as well as to notify him when the contractions became closer together. He knew she needed time alone.

He could not imagine what she must be going through. He recognized the despair in her eyes and knew the reason she lashed out had nothing to do with his proposal but was directed at the man who had betrayed her love.

She was going to give birth to her first child. This should have been a happy moment for her. A moment shared by her husband, her family, and others of those who loved her.

Instead, she was alone.

But she was not alone, and it was his task to assure her of the reality. He, Lady Tinsworthy, and all her friends at the hospital and Glen Castle were there for her. They might not be her family by birth, but they were her family by choice.

The day had turned to night as he strolled out onto the stone terrace near to the rooms Lady Elizabeth occupied. He had poured black coffee, knowing it would be a long night. With his free hand, he massaged the ever-present ache in his shoulder, a consistent reminder of the bayonet wound he had received, on a nameless battlefield in some godforsaken part of France, while fighting Napoleon.

When he had survived the attack, he awoke in a field hospital, near to the frontline, remembering he had wished to die alongside his comrades. Why had he survived and not them? He had asked the question of God and of anyone within earshot. His comrades were brave men, one and all, and deserved better than to die, let alone to do so far away from home and their loved ones.

He drank his black coffee under the serenity of a full moon, but his thoughts refused to rest. The night air was crisp and clean with the smell of cleansing rain in the air. It could wash away the blood on a battlefield, but not the memories.

Thomas rolled his shoulder again. He did not mind the discomfort. In fact, he welcomed the pain. It reminded him that despite his wounds he was alive, and grateful he could help the wounded as he had been helped. The skilled surgeon who made sure his wounds healed and never became infected had been one of the reasons he had become a doctor. But on days when he lost more lives than he saved, he wondered if he should seek another profession. The constant reminder of war and death tore holes in his soul.

The death of his wife, Agnes, who had blessed him with her love and with their child, Jonathan, was the deepest wound of all. The deepest guilt. That was the reason he was so concerned for Lady Elizabeth and her unborn babe. She was alone, and although he and Agnes had been married, he was not there to help her when she went into labor, a guilt he would carry to the last of his days.

Agnes always said she saw the kind heart and generous nature behind the mask he wore, and one day, she said, he would share it with the world. It was she who had suggested when he was recovering from his war injuries that he sell his officer's commission and study to become a doctor.

His prediction that his wife would not give birth for weeks was the reason he was so furious with Lady Montgomery's Doctor Merryweather. Agnes had gone into labor early and he had reached her only just in time to have her die in his arms.

"I thought I would find you here," Wilkes said, filling Thomas's half-empty coffee cup from a carafe, then filling his own. "I checked on Lady Montgomery. She is still in denial that the birth of her child is eminent." Wilkes pulled on his forelock. "Have you heard from your son's maternal grandparents? Tragic that your wife died bringing Jonathan into the world. How old is he?"

"Jonathan turned three last February. I visit him as often as I am able. His grandparents are good people, and my son is well cared for and deeply loved. I miss him dreadfully, but the experience in my youth taught me that a child needs a mother and father. He needs those he can count on, not a father who is rarely home and tied to his work."

Wilkes took a long pull on his coffee. "Your aunt's proposal of marriage to Lady Montgomery is not so preposterous an idea. It would solve two birds with one stone. Or in this case, a marriage certificate. A husband for Lady Montgomery and a mother for Jonathan. Marriage might also cause you to reevaluate the long hours you spend at the hospital."

"It would be a marriage of convenience," Thomas

said.

"Except you and Lady Montgomery are well acquainted and get on amiably—except for when she is in labor. Most *ton* marriages cannot boast such an accomplishment. This would be more than a marriage of convenience. It would be a marriage between friends."

"Except the lady in question will not have me."

Wilkes chuckled. "Well, there is that."

Chapter Fifteen

Elizabeth lay back against the soft pillows, eager for sleep. The drapes had been drawn to block out the damp evening air, a fire roared gently in the hearth, and less than half the branches of candles were lit. The golden glow created the atmosphere for a restful sleep. But she knew the attempt was useless.

As though in spite, her labor pains occurred at regular intervals, flouting Dr. Merryweather's inaccuracy at predicting the birth of her child. Mrs. Potter sat dutifully in a corner knitting, despite Elizabeth's attempts at getting her to leave and afford her privacy. Dr. Westerly had requested she stay and stay she would. Mrs. Potter's defiance of Elizabeth's request further irritated her.

Another pain rolled over her and she grimaced. She was aggravated with Dr. Westerly when all he had done was show her kindness. When Lady Tinsworthy had suggested she volunteer at the hospital in Merwood as a diversion, she truthfully had been skeptical. Due to the threat of contagion, her peers, herself included, preferred a doctor to come to their homes.

The strictest *ton* housekeeper would have been impressed with the level of cleanliness and organization in the doctor's hospital. In addition, Doctor Westerly cared for his patients and fought for their survival as though he were their personal protector. No, that was not entirely correct. He fought for them as though they were treasured family members.

Her real frustration lay not with Lady Tinsworthy or Dr. Westerly but firmly with her own gullibility. She had been swept away with the American captain's accent and the danger that swirled around him. He was different from any man she had ever met, and the thrill of the unknown had made her feel alive again. After her fiancé's death and her determination to bring his murderer to justice, she had felt as though she had been sleepwalking through life.

She had made a cake of things. She had gone on a whirlwind adventure with a man she barely knew, only to find herself about to give birth to a child out of wedlock.

Should she marry Dr. Westerly? The prospect seemed plausible. Her father and brother could hold their heads high, knowing that a dreadful scandal had been averted. Their daughter had married a lord, the brother of an earl. But would she be making a dreadful mistake? She might admire Dr. Westerly's dedication to his patients, but she did not love the man.

She respected him, and he was a pleasant sort, easy to talk to, and often sought out her opinions. He was without question handsome and well-formed. Any woman would welcome his attentions. But marriage?

Elizabeth heard Lady Tinsworthy's voice requesting an audience with Eliazbeth before she swept into the room like a winter storm. The silent Mrs. Potter set down her knitting, stood and curtsied to her ladyship as she entered.

"Dearest," Lady Tinsworthy addressed Elizabeth, "I have been granted permission from my nephew that, if I do not press my suggestion that the two of you wed, I am allowed to visit. Can you imagine a more impudent young pup?"

"I certainly cannot," Elizabeth said, joining Lady Tinsworthy in a hearty laugh. "And you love him all the more for his impudence."

"That I do." Lady Tinsworthy took Elizabeth's hands in hers. "I am very proud of the man he has become." Her ladyship acknowledged Mrs. Potter with a smile. "It is good to see you again, Mrs. Potter. I will stay with Lady Elizabeth. Would you be so kind as to bring us tea and biscuits? My nephew assures me it will be a long night."

Mrs. Potter bobbed a curtsy again, nodding toward Elizabeth as she left the room.

Elizabeth rubbed her belly to soothe another pain, frowning as she did so. "I had asked Mrs. Potter to leave, and she refused."

"My nephew left strict instructions that you were not to be left alone, and his orders are never questioned. I daresay he is not unlike a general on a battlefield."

"I am going to have a baby," Elizabeth said with a sob and a hiccup.

Her ladyship sat down beside the bed and patted Elizabeth's hand, rubbing it gently. "We know, dearest."

Elizabeth lifted her gaze. "I am not married, and I treated Dr. Westerly terribly. I am so ashamed. He did not deserve such treatment."

Her ladyship pulled the quilt higher on Elizabeth's belly. "My nephew is a good man and an exceptional doctor. He is aware that you did not mean what you said."

Elizabeth squeezed her eyes shut as a tear traveled

down her cheek. "I should marry him, shouldn't I?"

Lady Tinsworthy used a linen handkerchief to wipe the tear from Elizabeth's face. "This is your choice, dearest. When I talked with my nephew, he mentioned that he was agreeable to marriage. He is a kind and generous man. A man you can trust. And your heart is filled with pure love. My sincere wish for you and Thomas is that you will give love a chance to take hold and grow."

Mrs. Potter returned with tea and set the tray on a table beside the window. "Dr. Westerly informed me that he will return shortly to observe how Lady Montgomery is faring. How are we doing?"

"Mrs. Potter," Lady Tinsworthy said, standing, "we have a wedding to prepare. Please go down and inform the vicar and his wife. We have prepared for this happy turn of events, and they will know how to proceed."

****

A brief time later, Elizabeth's room was filled with vases of hydrangeas, and a bouquet of Rosa Desdemona lay on a table beside her bed. The white flowers with their delicate pink centers were tied with a soft pink ribbon, for the purpose of her holding them when she recited her marriage vows.

She had soaked through her nightgown again and Mrs. Potter was changing her into a loose-fitting white muslin gown overlaid with Belgian lace, provided by Lady Tinsworthy. Elizabeth thought with ominous clarity that this was her wedding day.

She had dreamed of this day, of the dress she would wear, the dazzling display of flowers, and the guests she would invite. Her marriage would take place in spring at St. George's on Hanover Street. Never in her wildest dreams would she have guessed her wedding would take place in a coastal village hospital.

A knock on the door admitted Lady Tinsworthy, followed by the Vicar Chesterfield, his wife, and Dr. Westerly.

"You look beautiful," Dr. Westerly said as he drew beside her, and Lady Tinsworthy handed her the bouquet of flowers. "Would you prefer to lie down?" When she shook her head, he wove his arm around her waist and took her free hand in his.

Elizabeth leaned against him as she clamped her teeth together, fighting through another wave of labor pains.

"We should make haste," Dr. Westerly said to Vicar Chesterfield. "This babe will not wait."

Through a fog of labor pains, Elizabeth overheard the vicar begin with the words, "Dearly beloved." The rest was lost as she fought to prevent crying out in pain.

Dr. Westerly said his vows, and she said hers. He slipped a gold band on the finger of her left hand, saying it had belonged to his father.

"I now pronounce you husband and wife," Vicar Chesterfield said.

Seconds later, pain shuddered through her body.

Dr. Westerly picked her up in his arms and carried her over to the bed. "Stay with me," he said. "We will do this together. I will never leave you."

Chapter Sixteen

Elizabeth gave birth to a beautiful baby girl.

Hours later, she awoke to the sound of rain rata-tat-tatting against her window, in awe of what had happened. She had a daughter. The curtains had been pulled back to display a harvest sun peeking out from behind slow-moving clouds. From the position of the sun, she guessed it was late afternoon.

Her daughter slept peacefully in a cradle beside Elizabeth's bed. Next to the cradle sat Dr. Westerly, fast asleep, slumped in a chair.

His elbow on the armrest, he had propped his head on his hand, while his other hand rested protectively on the baby's cradle. The scene tugged at her heart, and she swallowed down the lump in her throat.

It felt so natural, so right.

The hours she had been in labor seemed like a blur. What she remembered were the last words Dr. Westerly had said to her. *I will never leave you.*

She knew he meant the words. He was not the sort who lied or made false promises. She must not fall in love with Dr. Westerly, or worse, allow him to fall in love with her. Every man she had loved had either died or abandoned her. She must guard her heart, if only to protect them both.

The upturned hand Dr. Westerly had been resting his head on gave way suddenly. He jerked to a sitting position and rubbed his eyes. "You are awake," he said, blinking as though to clear the sleep from his eyes.

She smiled despite her resolution to protect her heart. "Your bedside manner is improving. But you look terrible."

A comfortable silence spread over the room, and Elizabeth knew how she reacted in this moment might define their relationship as husband and wife for all time. Could she risk it? Could she let down her guard and let him in?

The door to her room eased open, disturbing the silence. Mrs. Potter peeked around the door. "My lovelies. You are both awake. Would you like a tray brought up for the two of you?"

Dr. Westerly scrubbed his face with both hands. "Lady Elizabeth has informed me that I look terrible, and I will wager that was being kind. I need a bath, a shave, a change of clothes, and food. I will give her ladyship and her new daughter privacy and check on them both later."

"Oh, my," Elizabeth said. "I am in need of a bath as well. I must look a fright. Dr. Westerly." She smiled. "Thomas. We are husband and wife now. I shall call you Thomas and you must call me Elizabeth."

He grinned and gave the babe a kiss on the forehead, then paused for a moment, glancing toward Elizabeth as his grin spread into a smile. "You are wrong, Elizabeth, regarding your appearance. You have never looked more lovely to me than you do right now."

Chapter Seventeen

In late December, Thomas sat beside Elizabeth while she slept, listening to her breathe while he rocked the sleeping baby girl in his arms. A month and a half ago…had it really been that long? Her labor had lasted through the night and into the early morning hours. There had been times when he feared he would lose both mother and child, but Elizabeth's will to live was strong. He smiled, remembering when she swore like a seasoned sailor, cursing all men to a lifetime of suffering. Something about wanting them drawn, quartered, and then hung.

He smiled again, recalling when he had told his aunt that Elizabeth was extraordinary. He had not known at the time that his description had been prophetic.

Then Jane Marie had been born and Elizabeth's expression had been transformed into tears of joy and gratitude, and phrases like, "Isn't he the most beautiful baby boy you have ever seen?" had been uttered.

Thomas bent to place a gentle kiss on the baby's forehead. Elizabeth had named the child Jane, after her favorite author, Jane Austen, and Marie after her mother.

The quite domesticity of the moment brought a longing to hold his son, Jonathan, in his arms again. He had still not shared with Elizabeth the news that he had a son. He had sent a letter to Jonathan's grandparents that he had remarried and received a reply that they were expected any day. It has been a difficult letter to write to them. How would they feel about his remarrying? Would they believe he had betrayed the memory of their daughter? But the letter he received from them had been filled with love and good wishes for him and for Elizabeth.

He slid a glance toward Elizabeth again. The woman was breathtaking in repose: like one of the Greek or Roman goddesses. The revelation caught him by surprise, and he straightened, observing that Jane had awakened. The child stretched her little arms, formed her hands into tiny fists, and opened her mouth to yawn. Thomas knew a wail would come next. The little beastie had an insatiable hunger.

Thomas stood, rocking Jane gently, hoping to delay the feeding, thereby giving Elizabeth more time to rest. She had chosen to tend to Jane's needs herself rather than engage in the services of a wet nurse.

"Little Jane is awake," Elizabeth said, yawning in a similar manner to Jane's.

Watching her wake from rewarding sleep, her hair pleasingly unkempt, as though she had been making enthusiastic love, heated his blood. He imagined her hair falling in raven waves over the sides of her face, to settle on naked shoulders and caress breasts and nipples eager for his touch.

He adjusted his position in the chair. When had he stopped thinking of her as a friend and begun to imagine her in his bed?

She sat against the pillows, holding her arms for Jane. The small white buttons on her meadow-green nightdress were undone to allow her to feed Jane, giving Thomas a view of full breasts and blush-pink nipples.

"Sweet Lord," he said under his breath as he placed Jane in her arms gently, then turned his back toward Elizabeth with the pretense of folding one of Jane's blankets.

"Did you say something?" Elizabeth said to him.

Her question refocused him. "When you and Jane are stronger, we will leave Merwood for Glen Castle. My aunt is anxious to have you and Jane under her roof."

There was a long pause, and he knew she was not ignoring his statement but concentrating on smiling down at Jane while she helped her to latch onto her breast and feed. He heard a little chuckle. "I believe Jane must be the most adorable child ever born. Don't you agree?"

The joy in her voice pulled him to turn around, and he reveled in his view of her expression alive with the happiness of motherhood.

"I agree with you wholeheartedly," he said. "Jane is an exceptional child, in looks, temperament, and talent, and I will challenge anyone who questions our judgment."

She gifted him with a dazzling smile. "I too am anxious to return to Glen Castle. When we have a date confirmed, we should have a celebration in honor of Jane's birth. How many guests can your estate accommodate?"

"Enough worthy of a royal entourage. My aunt claims that at one time Glen Castle boasted that Henry VIII once spent the summer there. I have arranged for a doctor to take my place for a time so that I might spend more time with you and Jane. That doctor arrives within the week."

He knew he was stalling for time. His son and his wife's parents would arrive soon. He should have told

Elizabeth sooner. But the time had never seemed right.

"There is something I must tell you." He took a breath and plowed forward. "I have a three-year-old son." He paused again before he lost his nerve. "Jonathan and his grandparents are expected in a couple of weeks."

Her eyebrows pulled together as though she were deep in thought as she brushed her finger across Jane's cheek and an uneasy silence expanded. He knew she waited for him to fill in the gaps. She had every right to be angry with him. He was angry with himself for not divulging this information before they wed. It might have made a difference.

"I was married before, and Agnes and I had a child. Sadly, my wife died in childbirth."

Her eyes lifted to gaze intently into his. "Thomas, I am so sorry that your wife died giving birth to your son. I cannot imagine the pain of such a tragedy. That explains why you were so worried about me. If your son will arrive soon with his grandparents, within a fortnight, can I assume that Jonathan has been living with them?"

He nodded. "They are lovely people, and he is a happy lad."

"And you miss him," she said, smiling.

He heaved a sigh. "Every day. I should have told you sooner. I am not sure why I did not. I convinced myself he was better off with his maternal grandparents, who doted on him, rather than living with me. I told myself I was too busy to care for a child. An unpardonable excuse."

"Thomas. Please do not be so hard on yourself. You are a good man and thought of your son's needs before yourself. You have reached out for him now, and that is what matters." Jane had fallen asleep, and Elizabeth adjusted the babe in her arms, covering the child with a blanket. "My guess is that the reason they are visiting is that you wrote to them and told them you have married. They would assume you want Jonathan with you now you are wed. Am I correct?"

"You are a wise woman. Yes, that was my intent, but I was afraid to ask outright. I was not sure if they would give Jonathan up."

She held out her hand toward him. "You said they are lovely people. Of course they would want their grandson with his father. I am delighted that Little Jane has a big brother, and I am excited to meet him. Big brothers are such a blessing, although they can also be trying. My older brother teased me mercilessly when he discovered I was afraid of spiders. In retaliation, and knowing he was afraid of frogs, I placed one under his bedcover. After that incident we called a truce."

Thomas laughed and took her hand in his and kissed it. "I do not doubt it. Your brother realized he had met his match. What a wonderful story. Thank you."

"Whatever for?"

Keeping her hand in his, he moved beside her on the bed. "You could have been angry with me. Instead, you not only accepted that I have a son, but you also welcomed him. Thank you again. You mentioned your brother. We should invite him and your father to meet Jane and my son Jonathan. My aunt is anxious to host a party for us, especially when I told her that Jonathan might be coming to live with me at Glen Castle. She intends to invite all the residents within a ten-mile radius."

The warmth of his regard enveloped her. How easy it would be to lose herself in his gaze. She must not, her heart cautioned. She was a woman in a man's world. She had been deceived before and now it was not just herself but her daughter's welfare that she must protect. She must keep this man at a distance. It was the only way.

She slipped her hand from his and turned to her side, laying Jane next to her on the bed. "I am tired. I should rest while Jane sleeps." She winced at the harshness of her words as Thomas left and closed the door softly behind him.

"Oh Jane," she said. "What are we to do?"

Chapter Eighteen

Two weeks later, the carriage rolled along the ocean-view road at a steady pace toward Glen Castle, then turned inland to travel through a canopy of trees before once again traversing the cliffs. Elizabeth loved the winding road. She had only spent a short time at the castle, but she recognized the terrain and it felt like she was coming home. She wondered if that is how Thomas felt as well. He had been quiet all morning. He had decided to ride in the carriage with his son Jonathan, her, and Jane, rather than on his horse and sat opposite her lost in his thoughts.

She smiled to herself, glancing over at both father and son. Since Jonathan had arrived two days ago with his maternal grandparents, Thomas had not let his son out of his sight. They were inseparable as though they had never been apart. Jonathan lay nestled against Thomas' chest, sleeping soundly to the gentle sway of the carriage as it rolled along toward its destination.

She longed to strike up a conversation with Thomas but did not know how to start, or what to say. It felt like things had happened so fast. Less than a year ago she had been single. Now she was a married woman with two children. She smiled again at the sleeping boy and once again, her eyes brimmed with happy tears. The moment she met Jonathan, she considered him her son. She could not explain it, but it seemed that simple. One moment she had one child. The next moment she had two. She did not tell Thomas because she did not know how he would react, so she kept her feelings a secret.

She rocked the sleeping Jane in her arms and gazed out the window.

The last time Elizabeth had been here it had been in the long summer months, with their glow of sun-kissed beaches, warm days, and endless nights. Winter held a unique charm of its own. The air was crisp, the trees dusted with frost, and waves fringed with lacelike foam crashed against the cliffs. In many ways she preferred this time of year. It represented gathering around the hearth with family and, most importantly, the time of year when Little Jane had been born.

The weather had held, and except for moments when Little Jane had become fussy, wanting her nappies changed and a feeding, the short journey from Merwood to Glen Castle had been uneventful. Elizabeth glanced toward Thomas. He had received a letter from his aunt and afterward seemed as restless as the waves below. He was a complicated man she realized. Quite different than any man she had ever met and seemed genially interested in her opinion.

It was good that they traveled in silence. It allowed her time to reflect. She admitted she had a tough time accepting that she was a married woman. She had envisioned a fairytale-like experience where she was the beautiful princess who would meet her handsome prince, fall in love, marry, have children, dress fashionably, host lavish parties and live happily ever after. The reality had been nothing like the dream. Already, her life with Thomas had seemed more of a partnership than an endless string of entertainments.

But what would her father have thought of her choice?

Not surprisingly, her father had approved of her betrothal to the Duke of Conclarton. The duke had been the son of one of her father's friends—wealthy, handsome and intelligent, the perfect gentleman. Of course she would learn to love him, her friends would say. How could she not? He was the ideal husband. He was flesh and blood, not a hero from an Austen novel. It should not matter that Donald did not consider her his intellectual equal or asked her advice. But it had.

So, when he criticized Jane Austen's novels as frivolous nonsense, read by women with feathers for brains, she began to have doubts. But then she discovered he was also a code breaker for the Crown and believed the Austen novels would be perfect for the book cipher code he had been developing and asked for Elizabeth's help. She envisioned them working together and reconsidered. She was intrigued by the exciting and dangerous life he led and believed herself in love. But did she love the man, or the life he lived? He died before she had time to explore either possibility.

The carriage rolled over a rut in the road, jostling her back to the present. Thomas, who like Jane, had fallen asleep, straightened in the bench seat opposite her, and rubbed his eyes, sheepishly. He leaned back against the side of the carriage, holding the sleeping Jonathan on his lap. He had changed from the plain austere black suits worn by doctors to the more fashionable clothes titled gentlemen wore.

His jacket and breeches were understated in shades of dove gray, with a steel-gray embroidered waistcoat, white shirt, and expertly tied neckcloth. His Hessian boots had been polished to a high gloss before the five-mile trek from Merwood to Glen Castle. But then Jane had thrown up on Thomas's boots and Jonathan had used them like steppingstones to climb into his father's arms. Neither of which had bothered Thomas, which had pleased Elizabeth enormously.

"We have arrived," Thomas said, nudging the sleeping Jonathan awake. "I overheard you asking Mrs. Potter if her daughter would consider living at Glen Castle. Under the circumstances, a wise premonition. You will need a lady's maid as well as someone to help with the children."

Elizabeth smiled over at Jonathan as she secured a white knit bonnet, decorated with yellow rosebuds, on Jane's head. "Matilda Potter was overjoyed to help with the children. As far as a lady's maid," she said with a twinkle in her eyes, "I will need one. Whatever would women do without someone to help them dress? Why, we might resort to running naked in the streets wearing only our shoes, and ribbons in our hair."

He tore his gaze from the window to lift an eyebrow. "An interesting visual, I daresay. Do you really think the lack of a lady's maid would accomplish such a happy and scandalous outcome?"

She tapped him lightly on the arm. "You have missed my point. And stop smiling."

"I cannot. I keep envisioning women strolling through Hyde Park wearing nothing but their shoes."

"You are terrible."

He winked. "I am a man, after all."

She hid her own smile and bent over Jane in the hope of hiding her blush beneath her bonnet. She so enjoyed her exchanges with Thomas. "What did you mean when you mentioned a *wise premonition*?"

"My aunt informed me that many of our servants

have left. Ah, here we are."

The carriage broke through the canopy of trees to a clearing and rumbled through iron gates. When it rolled to a stop, Thomas jumped out. Two footmen in silver-and-black livery appeared. They bowed and greeted Lord Westerly as he disembarked and turned to help Elizabeth with the children.

The tallest of the two bowed again. "We received your missive, my lord, and the rooms for you and your wife and children are being prepared in the East Wing. We hope they meet with your approval." He paused, glancing toward the other footman. "It has been…"

The other footman stepped forward. "Begging your pardon, Lord Westerly, but her ladyship is most distressed. Your brother, the Earl of Willowdown, has hired at least fifteen or sixteen of our servants with the promise of increased wages. Lady Tinsworthy matched and then increased the Earl's offer, but it was to no avail. The housekeeper left suddenly. The cook as well," he added. "Those what left complained they disagreed with your aunt housing fallen women."

"The head housekeeper, and a number of the servants left?" Elizabeth said.

"Yes, it seems they have left for better employment," Thomas replied. "My aunt is understandably concerned." To the footman, he said, "If you do not mind my asking, why did you and your brother stay? I am sure the earl offered you a handsome inducement to leave."

"That he did, my lord. But we could not leave Lady Tinsworthy. She is a fine woman with a good heart for those who have been judged harshly. Mr. Fitzwilliam will have more on the matter. Here he comes now, my lord."

Mr. Fitzwilliam, looking as distinguished as he had when she left for Merwood close to six months ago, rushed down the stairs, adjusting his black waistcoat. One of the wolfhounds trotted along at his side. She recognized Finnegan as the same gray dog who had toppled over the tray of tea and biscuits she held when she was meeting with Lady Tinsworthy. The animal had grown as tall as his sire and stood higher than Elizabeth's waist. Finnegan stood obediently beside Mr. Fitzwilliam when he addressed Thomas. In a few short months, the dog had changed from an exuberant puppy to a sedate and obedient companion. Elizabeth was impressed.

"Lord and Lady Westerly, it is good to see you both at last. I trust you and your children had an uneventful journey from Merwood to Glen Castle?"

"We did, thank you, Fitzwilliam," Thomas said, scratching Finnegan behind the ear. "Would you mind showing Elizabeth and the children to their rooms? I wish to have a word with my aunt."

Mr. Fitzwilliam bowed and then grimaced. "Your rooms are not ready, my lord. Many of the remaining servants are working double shifts. Lady Tinsworthy knew you would understand that our priority lies with the care of her Ladies in Waiting. But I assure you that we will have your rooms ready within the hour."

With the mass exit of his staff, Elizabeth surmised that Mr. Fitzwilliam was making sure the rooms were ready for the lord and his family personally. When she first saw him descending the stairs, he had looked flushed and out of breath. She had believed it was due to his advanced age. Now she suspected another reason. No doubt he had not only overseen the cleaning but participated in it as well.

"If you do not mind," she said, "I would like to stroll in the garden until our rooms are ready. Jane, Jonathan, and I have been cooped up in that carriage and need fresh air."

When the men nodded, she headed to an overgrown path she had viewed from the carriage. Finnegan chose to leave Thomas and Mr. Fitzwilliam and trot along at her side, much to Jonathan's pleasure.

Through a break in the trees, she noted the path led to the castle's manmade lake where a willow tree's branches dipped below the surface of the water.

"Be mindful of the path," Thomas shouted. "And please do not go far."

"Do not worry," she shouted back. "If a highwayman tries to kidnap us, Finnegan will come to our protection."

She heard Thomas chuckle as she ducked her head under a low-hanging branch. Without meaning to, she stole a glance over her shoulder, only to find he was glancing her way as well. He gave a slight nod of his head.

She turned back to the path and smiled. Insufferable man.

There was not a cloud in the sky and the sun had decided to put in a much-welcomed appearance. A lovely day for a walk.

She glanced over her shoulder again toward Thomas, but this time he was conversing with Mr. Fitzwilliam. She would have loved to be a little bumblebee buzzing around them and catching snippets of their conversation.

Feeling Jane stir, Elizabeth adjusted her in her arms

and rubbed the child's back as Jonathan tossed pebbles into the lake beside the attentive Finnegan.

Thomas's brother had hired away a good portion of Lady Tinsworthy's staff, and just when Thomas was bringing his wife and family home to Glen Castle. Did the earl mean to embarrass his brother in front of his wife? That appeared a likely scenario. But the earl had also tried a similar tactic when he had forbidden the townspeople to work at Merwood Hospital. His scheme had failed, but that had not rendered it any less troublesome.

Elizabeth joined Jonathan and Finnegan by the water's edge. Jonathan held onto the fur at the nape of Finnegan's neck with one hand as he continued to toss pebbles into the lake. The sheer joy in the boy's expression chased away the gloom of her previous thoughts and with it the determination to discover what had caused the feud between Thomas and his older brother.

Chapter Nineteen

Elizabeth could not imagine a better reunion. The moment she entered Glen Castle, she was directed into the drawing room, where tea and small cakes were being served. Two of the new Ladies in Waiting, who introduced themselves as Miss Turnby and Miss Waverly, hurried over to meet the children, Miss Turnby asking if she could hold Jane, and Miss Waverly asking if it was okay for Jonathan to have cake.

With a nod to both and feeling relaxed for the first time in days, she smiled as Jane and Jonathan were fussed over as though they were royalty.

Margerie stood from her chair and swept Elizabeth in her arms. "You have arrived. I despaired that you would never come." She bent to tousle Jonathan's curls. "Elizabeth, who is this handsome lad? No, let me guess. This is Jonathan, Dr. Westerly's son. They have the same eyes."

Elizabeth laughed, taking Jonathan's hand. "They do indeed. It is good to be back. I have missed this drafty old place."

"Drafty?" Lady Tinsworthy said, holding out her hands toward Elizabeth as she approached. "How can you call this grand old lady drafty? She is a marvel."

"She is indeed," Mr. Fitzwilliam said, smiling, as he appeared from the hallway.

Lady Tinsworthy used her fan to swat the butler on

the arm. "You are impudent. Remind me why I have not fired you today?"

He wiggled his eyebrows. "The day is young, and you anticipate that I will yet prove myself indispensable."

Elizabeth took Margerie's arm and drew her to the side. "What is transpiring between these two since I left? They behave like young lovers."

"It happened soon after I gave birth to Charles. One of the chambermaids caught them in her ladyship's rooms. They were chasing each other around the room with a feather and they were both stark naked."

"Chasing each other? With a feather?"

Margerie nodded. "I know. Who knew either one of them could run?"

Elizabeth laughed so hard she snorted, then laughed again. "Did the maid say what they were doing with the feathers?"

Margerie grimaced. "No one wanted to ask. But ever since they were discovered they have been like you see them now. Inseparable and as giddy as two schoolchildren. We guess they have figured since everyone knew they were lovers it no longer mattered that they keep it a secret."

Elizabeth lowered her voice. "Quick, before anyone else joins us. Do you know anything about Dr. Westerly's brother, the Earl of Willowdown? Is it true that he has tried to hire most of Lady Tinsworthy's servants?"

"All true," Margerie said as she drew Elizabeth beside a corner window. "Lady Tinsworthy asked me to invite a Mrs. Scotchwich for tea in the village. She had been working here at Glen Castle for only a short while when she received the offer to work for the earl. She has a small child and was happy about the increased salary. But she said that Sedgwick House was not a happy place to work. The earl is drunk most of the time, and even when he is not visibly in his cups, he is morose. She said he must be an incredibly sad man. She believes she heard that he was seen stumbling through the corridors crying."

"Did Mrs. Scotchwich know why the earl was so troubled?"

"No one knows. Indeed, it is a great mystery. He is a handsome man, intelligent, and as wealthy as Croesus."

"And she never mentioned Dr. Westerly?"

"Only to say that everyone thought highly of Dr. Westerly. The older servants remembered a time when the two brothers were the best of friends. Their mother died when they were at university, but the change between the brothers occurred after Dr. Westerly married, and then worsened with the old earl's death a year later. According to Mrs. Scotchwich, the servants do not speak ill of him. Rather, they say he is a generous man and never raises his voice to them. They feel sorry for him and feel that he is in real pain."

Lady Tinsworthy joined Elizabeth and Margerie, reaching for both their hands. "I have good news. We are going forward with our Christmas Eve Ball. I am optimistic that all my ladies will find matches. I have invited every eligible bachelor within twenty miles. There is much to do, so I am pleased you are both here. Mrs. Potter sent word that her daughter will arrive tomorrow, and one of my Ladies in Waiting, a Miss Beverly Britten, has agreed to be Elizabeth's lady's maid until she gives birth in the spring. Come. We have much to do."

Chapter Twenty

A crescent moon reflected in the manmade lake outside Thomas's bedroom window as he observed trees swaying in the wind near the water's edge. It was the same body of water Elizabeth, Jane, and Jonathan had strolled near earlier today. Even as he dealt with the repercussions of his brother's interference, a smile from Elizabeth as she held Jane in her arms, and the laughter of his son as he played with Finnegan, placed it all into perspective. There was no place else he would rather be.

He understood theirs was a marriage of convenience. She had told him she did not love him. Why had that casual remark bothered him so? He was also aware that he had not thought through his growing fondness for Elizabeth. With even a marriage of convenience, the husband was entitled to marital rights, and—damnation!—he was only human. But he would not exercise those rights. He wanted Elizabeth to come to him by choice, not by duty.

His hands clasped behind his back as he gazed at the shadows darkening across the night sky. Today had been clear, a bluebird day, but a storm moved in and with it the promise of colder days and snow. As a young boy he had looked forward to the days when snow covered the hills and valleys. He, his brother, and their friends from the village would build snow forts, sled, and engage in snowball fights. As an adult, he knew the snow meant impassable roads that would make it difficult for new servants to find their way to Glen Castle. He longed for simpler times.

Thomas had assured his aunt he would find a solution to obtaining additional servants. Her primary concern centered around her Ladies in Waiting. Four additional ladies had joined the three already in residence. No one complained of the lack of servants, but that was likely to change.

He had been informed that yesterday his brother had left for the continent. As soon as the earl returned, Thomas would confront him. He had delayed it long enough.

Thomas turned from the window. A branch of candles on the table beside his four-poster bed, along with the glow of a fire in the hearth, cast the only light. The dim light suited him tonight. He was too tired to read. A brass bathtub had been placed in the center of his bedroom and steam curled over the edges. He stripped off his clothes and boots, lowered himself into the soothing water, and laid his head against the rim of the tub and closed his eyes.

As young boys, he and his brother had been inseparable. What would happen when they met face to face after almost five years? Would he receive an apology combined with the opportunity of a reconciliation, or would it be pistols at dawn?

When Thomas was first adopted and the Earl of Willowdown brought him to Sedgwick House to meet the family, it had seemed like a dream come true except for Lady Willowdown, who had been polite but distant.

On the other hand, Lady Tinsworthy, his brother's spinster sister, had opened her arms and declared

Thomas to be the child of her heart.

He sank lower into the water. He had never found fault with Lady Willowdown. He was old enough at the time to realize she had been placed in an impossible situation. As far as Thomas knew, the old earl had not consulted his wife. He had just brought home a bastard and ordered her to accept the young whelp as their second son.

The door to his chamber banged open.

Startled, Thomas straightened, sloshing water over the sides of the tub. "What is the meaning of this intrusion? I told Fitz I was not to be disturbed."

He pushed the hair from his eyes with both hands, trying to identify the intruder in the semidarkness.

Elizabeth moved out of the shadows of the doorway, more lovely than she had been this afternoon. She wore a long-sleeved cream-and-forest-green muslin dress, and her hair was swept to the top of her head in loose waves. He did not understand how she grew more beautiful each time he saw her, and with it his desire to have her in his bed. Propriety and good manners dictated that a gentleman rose when a lady entered the room. Under the circumstances, it would have been ill advised.

"Oh, I did not realize…" she said, her voice trailing off into a whisper. "We can speak in the morning at breakfast."

"Do not leave. The children—are they unwell?"

"No. No, they are sleeping. Mrs. Neverly, my friend Margerie, who helped at the hospital a few months ago, came into the nursery for a visit. Lady Tinsworthy was there helping me with the children at the time."

Thomas smiled, recalling the gossip he had overheard when he had taken Finnegan to the stables. "It seems my aunt and Fitz are lovers."

She took another step into the room. "They were caught chasing each other with feathers. That seemed so odd. What could they possible do with feathers?"

He chuckled again. "A few things come to mind."

She scrunched her eyebrows together. "Then you must tell me."

"I most definitely will not. You were about to tell me why you are here."

" Ah, yes. When I mentioned that I wanted to talk with you, your aunt suggested that she and Margerie should take care of the children. So, here I am." She retrieved a handkerchief from her sleeve. "Oh, my, but I am talking overly much. You are very naked."

"It would seem so," he said evenly. He smothered a grin, knowing that it might embarrass her more and he really wanted her to stay. She did not seem to be in a hurry to leave. Quite the contrary, as she took in her fill of him, which pleased him enormously. Then her gaze sped to his, and a becomingly rosy glow heightened the color in her cheeks.

"Your aunt assured me I would not be disturbing you. She mentioned that you catch up with your correspondence at this time of night."

Thomas chuckled, leaning back against the tub again. "My aunt is playing matchmaker, it seems. She is fully aware of everything that goes on at Glen Castle. She would know I had ordered a bath. Would you mind turning around while I dress? Sadly, my valet neglected to set out towels. Another interesting coincidence."

"A conspiracy is at foot," she said as she turned to face the door, still twisting the handkerchief in her hands. "The reason I wished to speak with you is that I plan to write to my father and brother, and it occurred to me that they will wish to know how we met. We should establish our story."

He stepped out of the tub and snagged his breeches. He sympathized with her dilemma. It was reasonable to assume her father and brother would want to learn the circumstances of how Elizabeth met her husband. "We could tell them we met at the hospital in Merwood."

"Mentioning the hospital might lead to other questions. No, I have thought this through. We met at one of Lady Tinsworthy's parties. You asked me to dance a waltz. It is the most romantic of dances and we fell in love at first sight."

"Impossible."

She glanced over her shoulder, then turned back quickly to the door. "You are still not fully clothed," she said. "You do not believe in love at first sight then?"

He reached for a shirt. Did he believe in love at first sight? An interesting notion. He conceded that when he first saw Elizabeth, from Dr. Merryweather's window, he had been attracted to her. She was a beautiful woman. But had he fallen in love with her on that first encounter or had it happened slowly and quietly? He believed it was a combination of the two.

He shrugged the shirt over his head and turned her to face him. "Love at first sight is for poets and dreamers. However, in our case it would explain the suddenness of our courtship, our marriage and that we have a child. I presume you intend to tell your family that I am Jane's father?"

She nodded and focused on what was now a twisted rope of linen. "You are correct. Love at first sight only happens in fairy tales, or Shakespeare's *Romeo and*

Juliet."

"Romeo and Juliet died tragically, and if I am not being disrespectful to Shakespeare, those two young lovers bungled the whole thing. Neither of them had to die. A colossal waste. If I loved a woman with as much passion as Romeo claimed to love Juliet, I would have defied her parents and spirited her far, far away."

Elizabeth lifted her gaze to his, smiling for the first time since she had entered his room. "And if I were Juliet and loved Romeo as much as Shakespeare wrote she did, I would have gladly gone with Romeo to the ends of the earth."

Chapter Twenty-One

Elizabeth stood by the nursery window, looking out at the pristine winter day and rocking the sleeping Jane in her arms as she relived her time with Thomas last night. Her legs felt a little wobbly and she refused to believe it had anything to do with seeing so much of the man unclothed. It was not as though she had never seen naked men before. Well, she had seen one naked man: the captain. But there was a world of difference between the two men, not just in appearance but in character. Thomas radiated not just physical strength but an inner strength that was difficult to measure. He filled any room he entered. Her whole body had reacted to him yesterday evening. She had ached for his touch and had not wanted to leave.

She laid Little Jane in the crib and knelt to button Jonathan's coat, longing for the time when he would call her "Mama."

"Can I really go outside, Lady Elizabeth?" Jonathan's eyes were as wide as twin saucers. "Mr. Fitzwilliam said it was too cold."

"Mr. Fitzwilliam worries over much. It is a delightful day to build snowmen."

"Or snow forts," Thomas added, entering the nursery.

Elizabeth stood, smiling, and shaking her head. "A snow fort? I was thinking more along the lines of snowmen and snowwomen. A quiet day of playing outside."

Thomas ruffled Jonathan's head of curls. "Well, lad, what say you? Are you in the mood for quiet and sitting around on our backsides, or for learning how to wage battle?"

Elizabeth laughed as she bundled up Little Jane and gathered her in her arms. "You are incorrigible, Dr. Westerly. What boy could resist a snowball fight?"

"You mean to take Jane with us? Isn't it too cold?"

"Now who is the worrywart? She is warm and snug, and besides, Jonathan will protect his sister against any snowballs that sail her way. Won't you, Jonathan?"

His face lit up as he nodded, tugging at Little Jane's blanket until Elizabeth bent lower so he could kiss her on the cheek.

"But first I promised Lady Tinsworthy that we would select a tree for the entry."

Thomas bowed, sweeping his hand in a dramatic fashion. "Your wish is my command. Shall we be on our way?"

A fleeting time later, Elizabeth was walking beside Thomas as they strolled down a wooded path into a snow-covered forest. Jonathan chased a little distance away, pointing at a squirrel that dashed out from behind a bush.

"Jonathan looks just like you must have looked at his age. He is so full of energy. I wonder what he will be like as he gets older?"

Thomas chuckled. "Full of mischief, I would expect."

"Then it is a good thing he has his father here to guide him," Elizabeth said. "He is also a truly kind child.

Did you see how gentle he was with Little Jane? Another trait he gets from you."

Thomas gazed toward Elizabeth. "You give me too much credit. It is true that Jonathan is a good lad and considerate of Little Jane. But it is due to his grandparents' influence. I was not around as much as I should have been. His mother, although he never knew her, was much like Jonathan's grandparents. She was soft spoken and never had an unkind word for anyone. On my part, I never considered myself kind when I was his age. Angry mostly."

She smiled at him. He was so humble. Was he not aware of the inner peace that flowed through him and calmed everyone in its path? She had not known him as a child or young man, but she would wager he was fair-minded and never resorted to bullying. That was not his nature.

"We will agree to disagree, sir. Did you know this is my favorite time of year?"

"Surprising," Thomas said. "I would have thought all ladies loved spring and summer."

"I am not most ladies, sir."

"That is something I am learning."

Jonathan pointed to a tall tree. "This one," he shouted. "I like this one."

"A fine tree," Thomas said coming up alongside the boy. "A good tree for climbing," he said, turning to Elizabeth with a wink.

She felt her face warm under his gaze, remembering the time when they first met. "I agree it is a fine tree. But first we need to make sure that birds and squirrels have not made this tree their home. Do you not agree?"

Jonathan looked toward Thomas with a questioning

stare. "What should we do, Papa?"

"Our snowball fight will have to wait until another day. Elizabeth is correct. We must make sure this tree is not a home for God's creatures." Thomas shed his outer coat and draped it over a limb. "There is nothing left to do. What say you, little man? Will you stand guard and protect your sister and Elizabeth while I climb the tree? But first, I need a boon from my fair lady. What say you to a kiss?"

She laughed, feeling her face warm again. "As impossible as it appears, a part of me believes that you planned this entire day to end just in this way. I must say yes, of course. We do need a Christmas tree."

"Yes, we do," he said.

Thomas cupped the side of her face and leaned to place a feather-soft kiss on her lips. A jolt of warmth, sweet with promise, caused her to return his gaze. "You are unexpected."

"And you are exactly as I expected."

Chapter Twenty-Two

Lady Tinsworthy entered the nursery. "I knew I would find you here. Your husband has gone to the Merwood hospital, and I am here to take you on an outing."

"You are generous. However, I am perfectly content with the children."

"I offer a compromise. We can take them with us. I have a wagonful of food and clothes to deliver to the Vicar Chesterfield in Merwood. You must come."

"It might be good for the children to have an outing, and I was looking forward to browsing in the bookstore."

"That is the spirit. We have only one detour along the way."

An hour later, Lady Tinsworthy's coach, followed closely by a wagon of food and clothes for those in Merwood, rolled to a stop at a stately Georgian mansion.

"Who are we visiting?" Elizabeth said.

"My nephew, the Earl of Willowdown. Prepare yourself. He has been out of sorts of late."

"Are we expected?"

"Of course not. What would be the fun of that?"

True to her nature, Lady Tinsworthy insisted she be allowed to enter and that yes, indeed, she would mind waiting for her nephew.

Elizabeth rocked Little Jane in one arm and patted the space beside her on the settee for Jonathan to join her.

He scrambled up beside her, taking a deep breath, which in a three-year-old meant he was immensely bored.

"I'm hungry," he said, crossing his arms over his chest and leaning against the settee.

"Of course you are dearest," Lady Tinsworthy said. "I am as well. Where is the servant with the tea? Ah, here he comes now. You are in for a treat. My nephew's cook, a Mrs. Nettle, is known for her cakes and jams."

The servant set a tray of tea and thin slices of apricot cake on the table beside Elizabeth.

"To what do I owe the pleasure of your *surprise* visit, Aunt?" said a man at the doorway. The slender man leaned on a cane and appeared haggard, and although his tan breeches, white hose, and black embroidered vest were well tailored, they looked as though he had slept in them.

Lady Tinsworthy rose from the settee with a nod. "Can't your aunt visit her nephew without his thinking there is an ulterior motive than familial love?"

He cast her a lopsided grin as he limped into the room, relying heavily on his pearl-handled cane. "You always have more than one reason for what you do, dear aunt. That is the one constant upon which I can rely. And who do we have here?" he asked, having turned to gaze at Elizabeth, Little Jane, and Jonathan.

"I apologize, Harry. I have been remiss. May I introduce your brother's wife, Lady Westerly, their daughter, Jane, and your brother's son, Jonathan."

"Agnes's boy," Harry said with a catch in his voice. "He looks like her." He straightened, leaning on his cane with both hands and bowing to Elizabeth. "It is a pleasure to meet you."

"And I you," Elizabeth said, with a seated

equivalent of a curtsy. She was used to the formality of the *ton*, but the air between them was strained.

He bowed again. "You are all welcome to stay as long as you wish, but I must excuse myself. I have a prior engagement that cannot be postponed."

"We would like to invite you to dinner," Elizabeth said. She knew the moment she said the words that she had overstepped. Glen Castle belonged to Lady Tinsworthy, and Elizabeth had not discussed the matter with her.

An uncomfortable silence grew as Jonathan slipped from the settee to toddle over to the earl. The boy tilted back to gaze at the tall man. "Does your leg hurt?"

The silence grew as the earl and the boy continued to stare at one another. Little Jane yawned in Elizabeth's arms, then nestled back to sleep.

"Yes, it does. You are an observant young man, and like your father. You have his eyes."

The earl raised his head, swallowing as he bowed again. "Aunt, I am glad you came, and Lady Westerly, I will consider your kind offer. Good day to you."

When they were once again in the carriage and traveling to Merwood, Elizabeth turned toward Lady Tinsworthy. "I apologize if I overstepped when I invited the earl to dinner."

"Nonsense. I should have done so myself. Well, I do believe that our visit went well."

"I know Thomas is adopted, but I was struck by how much alike they look."

"Do they, dear?" Lady Tinsworthy said, staring out the carriage window. "I never noticed."

Chapter Twenty-Three

A week later, Thomas descended the back entrance staircase, taking the steps two at a time. "Devil take it," he swore. His wife and aunt had invited his brother to dinner. What had possessed them? And how had they learned before he had that the earl was back in Merwood? The whole matter was beyond the pale.

He planned to go in to the hospital this morning, but first he had a stop to make. Sedgwick House was only a short distance from Merwood. Over the past few years, he had avoided traveling in that direction, but he had to do something about his brother, Harry. Failing to disrupt operation of Merwood hospital, the earl had turned his sights on Glen Castle, and he had almost succeeded.

Bloody hell. What had Thomas done to cause his brother's vengeance?

The weather, with its earlier promise of sunshine and clear skies, had descended into a gray day with the smell of rain in the air. He and his aunt had been successful in luring the servants back, but it had been tough going, and they were still in need of additional staff and contractors to help with the repairs. What the earl had done was inexcusable.

Thomas could not for the life of him understand what had caused this rift between them. They had been more than brothers. They had been best friends. But a path of reason and civility had to be forged.

His groom waited while Thomas secured his doctor's bag, mounted his horse, and headed in the direction of Sedgwick House. After his brother's abominable behavior at Thomas and Agnes's wedding breakfast four years ago, Thomas had vowed never to return. But they lived near one another, besides the fact that the earl had involved the whole town of Merwood in his feud. Wars between families had started on far less. Thomas did not have a choice. He must find a path forward.

After his visit with his brother, he planned to see his patients and, God willing, return home in time to play with the children before dinner. If fortune shone on him, he and Elizabeth would have time for a quiet moment. He enjoyed her company, even when they sat by the fire and read in silence or strolled in the woods around the castle. Her grasp of topics from politics to literature impressed him and stretched him to become a better student himself. She grew more beautiful to him every day. She talked of London, of what it offered, and that she missed attending the theatre.

Her last comment troubled him.

Did it mean she longed for her life in London and had tired of life in the country?

What would he do if she told him she would prefer to live in London? It was common for married couples to live separate lives. Until he met Elizabeth, he had thought that sort of life would suit him. She would have her friends and entertainments in London, and he would oversee the hospital in Merwood. But now he realized that without his family his life would be a meaningless existence.

Nothing came to mind. He would not offer money

as an inducement. He wanted her to stay because that was her choice.

He took the bend in the road that led under a canopy of trees to Sedgwick House. The mere thought of being separated from Elizabeth and his children chilled him as though a wild wind from the north had swept over him. He shivered as he approached the circle entrance that led to his brother's estate. What could he do to stop her if she told him she would leave?

Thomas dismounted and turned his horse over to a footman dressed in gold-and-white livery. Sedgwick House was built with a nod to Greek and Roman architecture. Marble pillars and wide staircases adorned the whitewashed stone structure.

As he reached the top step, the door opened and a butler, in a dark suit with a white shirt and collar as starched as his austere expression, gave a slight bow.

Thomas did not recognize the man, and he did not have to be a Romani Gypsy fortuneteller to guess the butler's thoughts as the man looked Thomas from head to toe and found him wanting. Thomas should have taken better care of his clothes before meeting the earl. Even when riding in the country, a gentleman looked the part of a rich and titled lord, especially when one expected an audience with a man with as lofty a title as his brother. The saying that the clothes made the man was not an idle expression. The cut of a man's clothes signaled his rank, position, and wealth. Many of his class went into debt to dress fashionably.

"Lord Thomas Westerly to see the Earl Willowdown," Thomas said. "You can inform his grace that his brother wishes an audience. And you are?"

The butler bowed. "Mr. Shepley, milord. We noted

your approach. If you would be so kind as to wait a moment in the drawing room, I will inform his grace."

The butler stepped aside, allowing Thomas entry.

The Greek theme of the outside had been extended into the interior. Life-sized Greek statues of robed politicians stood guard near the winding marble staircase. On the high ceiling, a mural portrayed the god Prometheus, who had defied the Olympian gods by stealing fire from them and giving it to humanity in the form of technology, knowledge, and civilization. Thomas's father, a respected member of the House of Lords, had commissioned the mural with the idea of inspiring his sons to respect education, and the plan had worked.

Thomas followed the butler inside and to the drawing room, which should more aptly have been called the Gold Room. The furniture, walls and cornices were gilded, and the chandeliers painted with gold leaf. During the spring and summer months when the drapes were drawn to allow in the sunshine, the room blinded visitors with its light.

Their mother had preferred receiving guests in here, saying that it reminded her of the apartments in the homes frequented by Queen Charlette and thus gave Sedgwick House a regal appearance. Their father, on the other hand, preferred the library.

Thomas expected his brother to be in residence at this time of year. The earl would have exhausted the good will of his acquaintances in London by now, as well as tired of his mistresses. December and January were his brother's months to start fresh. New friends. New mistresses.

Shepley entered the drawing room. "The earl will

see you in the library, my lord. If you will follow me."

"I'll find my way, thank you, Shepley."

"But my lord…"

He waved away Shepley's concern. "Do not worry. I will inform the earl that I pushed you aside and you had no choice but to allow me to pass."

Thomas had no trouble finding the library, but his brother was nowhere to be seen. Still, as a child both he and his brother had spent happy hours reading books there regarding adventure and travel, so Thomas selected a translated version on the exploration of Marco Polo in China, a volume their father had purchased for them when he learned of their shared passion for travel. According to popular lore, Rustichello da Pisa had written the travelogue from accounts told to him by Marco Polo while they were both in prison in Genoa.

"I had forgotten we still had that old book," the earl said, entering from the adjoining room. "To what do I owe the pleasure?"

Thomas spent another moment before he closed his book and turned, knowing it irritated Willowdown to wait. He heard a woman's whispered voice and the scent of a heady perfume. No doubt the earl had brought his newest mistress along with him.

The earl directed a large-bosomed woman with dyed red hair—and wearing a low-cut, deep purple gown more suited to the bedroom than a ballroom—to the bank of windows at one side of the room. She sat on a gold embroidered wingback chair and swung her bare leg over the armrest, smiling seductively toward Thomas. Her heavy makeup covered either advanced age or youthful appearance. Thomas could not discern which, and whatever the reason, the result rendered her a caricature.

When he and his brother attended university together, his brother had preferred women with delicate features who wore little or no makeup or adornment and only gentle, pastel colors. This woman lounging on the chair held none of those attributes.

The earl had not aged well in the years since they parted ways after a contentious argument at the wedding breakfast at Sedgwick House that had included threats and name-calling. The earl had accused Thomas of stealing the affections of the woman he loved. Willowdown's complexion showed the result of late nights of drink and debauchery. He remained trim, however, but he walked with a limp that appeared to pain him.

Willowdown poured himself a whiskey from a crystal decanter. "Have you met my newest mistress? Monique, meet my brother, Lord Thomas Westerly, although he prefers the moniker of *Doctor* Westerly. He has opened a hospital for the poor in Merwood. His virtues know no bounds."

"The pleasure is all mine," Monique purred in a fake French accent.

"When you tire of your wife, I will gladly share Monique. Call it a wedding gift."

"Even if I were not a married man, Willowdown, your offer would hold no appeal."

Willowdown laughed bitterly, sipping his whiskey. "I forgot. Monique, my brother has the unique distinction among the gentlemen of the *ton* to have never paid for sex and believes in fidelity after marriage."

"There was a time, brother," Thomas said, "when that description applied to you as well."

Willowdown finished his whiskey in one swallow.

"That was a long time ago."

Regret laced the earl's voice, and the realization caused Thomas to reassess his brother's motivation. The man harbored a deep wound, and it bothered Thomas that he had not recognized it before. He had thought the worst of his brother without questioning what had caused their rift.

"Why did you conspire to hire away our aunt's servants?" Thomas said. "You must have known she would be hurt, believing you resented her for some reason."

"Direct and straight to the point, as always. You really must acquire the talent for small talk, my good man." The earl pressed the heel of his hand to his forehead. "I never considered how it would hurt her. I only thought to cause you trouble and embarrassment, and so I convinced myself the journey to the edges of what is considered Christian was worth the loss of what was left of my soul. I was mistaken. I still have a conscience. I deeply regret what I did. What a bother." He poured himself another drink with an unsteady hand. Amber liquid sloshed over the sides of the glass as he lifted it to his lips. "You have married again, with a new wife, an heir, and a daughter. Well, done, brother. As well, you have opened a hospital in Merwood." He raised his glass to Monique. "We must toast my brother. He is a wonder. Our father would be proud of you and sorely disappointed in me."

Was this the wound that would not heal? Did his brother feel their father would have been disappointed with the man Harry had become?

Mentally Thomas recapped their life together. Their father had showered praise on his sons equally. Unlike many fathers of the *ton*, their father did not believe in the whip or the switch to discipline his sons. A single look of disapproval, followed by a lengthy discussion on the merits of their action, always proved effective.

"I am sure you are mistaken," Thomas said. "Our father was proud of you as well." Thomas had come here to fight, but when he saw Willowdown and the depths to which his brother had fallen, all Thomas felt was concern. "What happened to you?"

"You happened," Willowdown said, slurring his speech. "I loved Agnes and wanted her as my wife."

"You never told me you were fond of Agnes. If you had told me, you loved her, I never would have courted her. You have my word."

Harry groaned, rubbing his leg. "Please inform your wife that I cannot accept her dinner invitation. You should…"

Harry slumped to the ground.

Monique screamed as Thomas rushed to his brother.

"My God! You are burning up!"

"Let me be. It is my leg. It will heal. I fell off my horse."

"I heard a scream," Shepley said, running into the library.

"Shepley. Get my doctor's bag from my horse."

"I am not your concern," Harry said. "Leave me."

"The devil take it. You *are* my concern. You are my brother."

An hour and a half later, Thomas approached his brother's bedchamber and eased open the door. Dr. Wilkes stood beside his brother, talking with him about hunting.

After examining Harry, Thomas discovered that his

brother's right leg had been broken when he fell from his horse, and a couple of his ribs were broken, as well. Considering his injuries, no wonder Harry had been in so much pain. Thomas had put the leg in a splint and had sent for Wilkes and Mrs. Potter. His brother had insisted on his own sawbones, a Doctor Calaway.

He had had Wilkes watch over his brother while Thomas had made arrangements at the hospital for a local doctor to cover his patients while he cared for his brother. He had also sent a message to Elizabeth and his aunt at Glen Castle keeping them up to date on Harry's condition.

Now, Thomas asked, "How is my brother doing, Wilkes?" He used the wash basin on the table to cleanse his hands. "And where the devil is Dr. Calaway?"

"The earl has improved, despite Calaway's interference. He brought out his jar of leeches and wanted to bleed your brother. I sent him on his way. Mrs. Potter sent word that she will arrive this evening."

"Good man. You can leave us. I will take over from here."

The door closed behind Thomas as he felt his brother's forehead. His fever had broken.

"I'm glad Wilkes dismissed that quack," his brother said. "Never liked the man. It was Shepley who sent for him, to begin with." Harry laughed, then coughed. "That hurt."

"Do not laugh. Just point to where it hurts."

"Bossy," Harry said, pointing to his rib cage on his left side, then wincing.

"You also cracked a rib in the fall. Try not to move too much." The color in Harry's skin looked normal and he was in good spirits. All good signs.

"I anticipated that you might have cracked a rib or two and bound your chest out of precaution. "Your ribs and leg will heal. Willowdowns are a tough lot. Remember the time when you climbed that tree and fell and broke your arm? The doctor said the break was so severe you would never use that arm again."

"You were all of twelve years old, but you had the stones to call the man a quack."

"I did, and we proved him wrong. What you need now is to rest and heal."

"Lady Westerly is exceedingly kind. You are a lucky man. I need to tell you something."

Thomas covered his hand over his brother's. "The only thing you need to tell me is that this feud between us is over. You must believe me when I say I never knew that you had feelings for Agnes. If I had, I would never have courted her, let alone married her."

Harry slid his gaze toward the windows in his room, where sunlight filtered through the panes. "You are an honorable man. I always knew that would have been the case if you had known. The truth was…" Harry turned once more toward Thomas. "The truth *is* that I courted her, and she rejected me. Imagine. I was the heir to a dukedom, and she rejected me. She loved you, not me."

"Harry, even so, had I known how you felt, I never would have married Agnes. I only have one brother." His throat clenched. "My children need their uncle and I need my brother. Your father treated me like his flesh and blood, and you did the same. But I never knew my natural mother and father and why they abandoned me. All orphans want to believe that the parents who abandoned them had a good reason. But that is just a lie we tell ourselves to be able to forgive them. I am only

144

telling you because I want you to know how grateful I am that your father adopted me and that you are my brother."

Harry reached for Thomas's arm and drew him nearer. "It is not my place to say. But ask Lady Tinsworthy. She knows the truth about your mother and father."

Chapter Twenty-Four

At Glen Castle, the warm aromas of freshly baked bread, roasted lamb and little potatoes drifted into the dining room as servants entered in single file to serve the guests. More ladies had arrived in the last few days, and the room was filled with the hum of conversation and introductions.

When the guests were seated, servants began serving while footmen poured red wine into crystal goblets.

"The food smells delicious," Elizabeth said to Margerie. "Has Lady Tinsworthy hired a new cook?"

Margerie smiled and mouthed a thank-you to the footmen who served her a plate of sweet and savory dishes. "Miss Brown returned late last night. She said she trained a girl from Merwood to take over her duties at the hospital. She missed us, but if you ask me, it was the handsome footman Mr. Fitzwilliam just hired that caught her eye. How is Dr. Westerly's brother? Lady Tinsworthy mentioned that he had broken his leg."

Elizabeth cut a bite-sized piece of her lamb. "The earl is doing very well, and Thomas sent me word that he means to bring his brother to Glen Castle." She smiled down as she speared a little potato. "I received a letter from my father. He congratulates me on my marriage and the birth of Jane and mentioned that the reason he had not written sooner was because he was struggling with gout."

Margerie sipped her wine. "Your father and Lady Tinsworthy have that in common, although she is doing better of late. She alternates between cursing and accrediting her nephew on the change, as he gave the servants a list of forbidden foods."

"I will be sure to let my father know. He plans to arrive before Christmas but mentioned my brother had to postpone a visit to meet his new niece until after the first of the year. And on other news, Thomas said he does not want to leave his brother, but he misses his family."

Margerie nudged Elizabeth with a grin. "He misses you. I also have news. I received a curious letter from my pirate. It was very strange. He went on and on about saying he felt like the adventurer Marco Polo when he met someone by the name of da Pisa. What do you think it could mean?"

Elizabeth set her fork down. "When Lady Tinsworthy and I visited the earl, I noticed a copy of a book written by Marco Polo in the earl's library. Marco Polo met a man by the name of da Pisa when they were both imprisoned in Genoa. Your pirate could be trying to send you a coded message. Prisoners' letters are read before they are posted. I could be wrong, but I believe that your pirate is in prison and his letter was his way of asking for help."

Margerie wiped her mouth with her linen napkin. "I would never have made that connection. You are brilliant. I will make the arrangements to travel to Italy in the morning."

"You would have figured it out in time. I am only speculating. Did I overhear Lady Tinsworthy mention that Miss Brown had prepared apple pie with cream for dessert?"

Margerie pressed her hand to her heart. "My very favorite."

Elizabeth concentrated on cutting more of the lamb on her plate. Unfortunately, she had lost her appetite. She had received two letters this afternoon, one from her father and the other from Lord Stewart Bronson. Lord Bronson had worked with her fiancé on many clandestine missions at the time of her fiancé's death, and in his letter his lordship invited her to live in London and take over where her fiancé had left off.

God help her. The allure was appealing.

Chapter Twenty-Five

Well after midnight, Elizabeth heard Little Jane crying in the adjoining room. Matilda had taken her for the evening so Elizabeth could get some sleep. She had not been sleeping well. She missed Thomas and the notion was mad because they did not sleep in the same room, let alone the same bed. But knowing that he was at Sedgwick House, not Glen Castle, with no idea when he would return, bothered her more than she cared to admit.

She felt the worse for her selfishness because he was where he should be. He was caring for his brother.

She swept the covers aside and slipped from the bed in only her nightdress.

Then, miraculously, Little Jane stopped crying. Elizabeth yawned, debating whether she should try to go back to bed or check on her child. But she knew she would not be able to sleep. Since as long as she could remember, she could never go back to sleep, no matter what time she awoke.

Her waist-length hair had twisted free of its single braid, so she flung it over her shoulders as she yawned and moved into the adjoining room.

But her daughter was not alone, nor was she asleep. Jonathan lay curled on his trundle bed and Thomas was holding the smiling babe in his arms, rocking the child back and forth as he talked to Jane softly. Jane gazed toward Thomas in rapt attention as though whatever he was saying was the most momentous and essential information she had ever heard.

Elizabeth's eyes misted as she leaned against the doorjamb. Thomas was home. The realization struck her that, from the very first moment, Thomas had accepted her daughter into his life as though she were his own flesh and blood. There had never been any question. Thomas had embraced fatherhood as though he was born to it.

Perhaps being orphaned had taught him the value of family. Or that was just who he was. Being orphaned and not adopted until he was an older child might have turned him bitter and angry. He had not shared that part of him, although she hoped that someday he would. But if he had struggled, he had found his way out of that deep well and emerged to become the loving man she saw before him.

He turned, a smile lingering over his lips. "There is your mama, Jane. Doesn't she look pretty? Should I tell her I have taught you how to blow bubbles just like I did your big brother?"

"I did not expect you home so soon." She pushed away from the doorjamb, as warmth spread over her at Thomas's comment. "Bubbles? What a talented babe. Let Mama see?"

"I could not stay away, so I brought him with me. I did not want to wake you, and when I heard Jane, I could not help myself."

"Your brother is here as well?"

He nodded. "My aunt had rooms made up for him, and he is sleeping as soundly as Jonathan."

She moved to stand beside him, her body close against his. "Where is Matilda?"

"I told her she was no longer needed. Papa was here."

Thomas had said the word "papa" softly, as his eyes searched hers. He was asking permission to be Jane's father not just in name only, a turning point in their relationship. She could chastise him for referring to himself as Jane's father. She did not doubt he would never retreat from Jane, even if she would not allow him to refer to himself as Jane's father. The realization warmed her heart. Most men would not have embraced fatherhood in such a manner. In a comparable way, she longed for Jonathan to call her Mama, but she would not insist. The gentlemen she knew considered fatherhood a duty to continue their line. Affection for one's children was rare.

She brushed the back of her fingers over Jane's cheek lightly. "Well, little one, your father tells me he has taught you how to blow bubbles. Can you show me?" She smiled down at the sleeping babe. "Later, little one, you can show me what your papa taught you." She lifted her gaze to Thomas's. "You have worked a miracle. Jane is asleep."

"I like your hair like that," he said, his voice whisper soft.

Her hand rose to comb through the tangled mass of curls. She must look a fright. What could the man be thinking? Her hair had not only come loose from its single braid but, because of its unfashionably unruly curls, it stood out in all directions.

"You are being kind. I must look a fright."

Thomas's gaze had not faltered as he slowly shook his head. "Never in my eyes."

His remark and the unguarded and passion-filled

look in his eyes took her by surprise. A man had never looked at her in that manner before. Her face warmed under his gaze. "I have been told, on more than one occasion, that hair like mine is a lack of order and evokes chaos."

He reached for a strand and brought it closer. "Your hair smells like a rose garden."

"Rose water," she said with a lump in her throat. "I wash my hair in rose water."

"Ah, that is the fragrance I smell. The men in your life are fools. Your hair does not evoke chaos. It symbolizes a free spirit full of passion and love."

"Thomas…"

The baby was asleep in his arms as he bent to kiss Elizabeth, his touch as light as a summer breeze.

Chapter Twenty-Six

The next morning, the ballroom was in a state of upheaval as Elizabeth sidestepped a box of decorations on her way to breakfast. Chandeliers had been pulled down for dusting, window coverings removed, and a good portion of the furniture and rugs taken away. In the center of the room, workers were positioning a tall fir tree in place while servants unpacked crates of oranges, apples, candles, holly, and ribbons that would be used to decorate the tree.

Christmas Eve was only a few days away, and after breakfast she fully intended to help decorate the tree and build wreaths and kissing balls out of mistletoe.

The oak dining table, instead of holding a prominent position in the center of the breakfast room, hugged the far wall adjacent to the buffet table. A veritable parade of servants brought silver trays laden with savory and sweet breakfast foods whose variety and smell tempted the most selective pallet.

An ice-blue winter sun shone into the room from the windows and glass doors that opened out onto a terrace. Warmth from the fireplace did its best to chase away the morning chill, but winter had arrived last night and cast a blanket of snow and frost over Glen Castle.

The first to arrive for breakfast, Elizabeth paused beside the window to drink in the view. She looked forward to talking with Thomas. She had delayed it long enough. Their main topic of conversation would be centered around the children. She loved them both dearly, but something tugged at her thoughts and would not relinquish its hold.

She patted the letter she kept in her pocket. It was the one she had received from Lord Bronson a day or two ago. It had been flattering and begun with complimenting her on her part in the capture of her fiancé's murderer. The letter ended asking her if she would consider moving to London and working for the Crown as a code breaker as her fiancé had.

The whole notion was preposterous. She was a wife and mother, and her life was in Merwood. She could not deny that she was flattered. Few women of her station were asked to do more than look fashionable, as though they had little more than a sixpence of sense. Of course she would tell Lord Bronson she could not possibly. But first she would have to tell Thomas about the offer. She would not want him to somehow find out about it on his own.

Elizabeth overheard Lady Tinsworthy talking to someone in the hallway.

"Thomas," Lady Tinsworthy pleaded as she entered the breakfast room, wringing her hands. "Let me explain." Then a door slammed.

Lady Tinsworthy strode into the breakfast room, then halted when she saw Elizabeth. "Oh! I thought the room was empty. The breakfast looks delicious. Miss Brown is a blessing."

"This is not Miss Brown's doing," Elizabeth said. "She and Mrs. Neverly left early this morning for Genoa."

"Yes, I had forgotten." Lady Tinsworthy said

absently, as she brushed her cheek and crossed to the buffet table. Instead of selecting there, however, her shoulders hunched over and she sobbed. "I am such an old fool!"

Elizabeth rushed to her side. "What is wrong? I overheard you and Thomas quarreling."

"By now the whole castle will have overheard what Fitz and I worked hard to hide."

"You do not have to tell me."

Lady Tinsworthy sank onto a chair a servant had pulled out for her. "You will hear of it soon enough. Fitz and I are Thomas's natural parents. I tried to explain that we did not place him in the orphanage. I was so young, and Fitz was…well not suitable. We planned to run away together. My father discovered our plan and was livid. I have never seen him so angry. He threatened to have Fitz arrested. I promised I would stay if he did not bring charges against Fitz and found our child a good home. Then years after Thomas was born, we learned that my father had placed our son in an orphanage." Her voice broke on a sob. "Thomas tells me he cannot forgive us for abandoning him."

Elizabeth's heart raced as she placed her arm around Lady Tinsworthy's shoulders. Elizabeth had only been a mother for a short span of time, but she could not imagine the pain of giving up your child. The pain would be excruciating. But Thomas suffered as well. He believed his parents did not want him and that is why he had been abandoned. Learning to forgive would take time for them all.

Lady Tinsworthy was correct. This news would spread through the castle like wildfire. A group of Ladies in Waiting, in various stages of their pregnancy, entered the room at that moment, all talking at once.

"Where is Thomas?" Elizabeth asked. "I could talk to him. Tell him how much it hurt you to give him up."

"You are kind," Lady Tinsworthy replied, "I believe he headed in the direction of the stables. But this is not your concern. This is my doing."

Elizabeth kissed Lady Tinsworthy on the cheek. "You have been there for everyone. It is time someone was there for you."

Elizabeth grabbed her outdoor coat, gloves and bonnet and braced for the wind as she marched toward the stables. She had no idea how she could make this right, but she had to try.

"What are you doing here?" he asked, holding the reins of his horse as he emerged from the stables just as she arrived. His voice was strained and laced with pain. "If you are here, it must mean that you overheard my conversation with my aunt. Or should I say, mother," he said bitterly. "Did she tell you that she abandoned me, and that Fitz is my father?"

Pain rolled over him in waves. She wanted to reach out to him and gather him in her arms. Instead, she blew on her gloved hands to warm them. "I am so sorry. I cannot begin to understand what you are feeling, or if you can ever forgive them. But know that whatever you do, I am here."

He stroked his horse's mane. "I wish I knew what to do. It is all jumbled up inside. Rationally, I know they had their reasons. She was unbearably young at the time. Barely seventeen or eighteen. Fitz was a servant."

"She told me that her father wanted to have Fitz arrested."

He looked toward her. "She did not tell me that part.

Her father was a lord, wealthy and powerful. He could have said anything about Fitz and would have been believed."

"Her father told her if she did not run off with Fitz, he would find you a good home. She believed him."

"Bloody hell. My grandfather was a piece of work."

She believed her father had found you a loving home."

His horse nudged him in the shoulder and Thomas rubbed the horse's neck. "Easy boy. We will take that ride I promised in a short while. "Secrets. It is a miracle they were able to keep this from me for so long."

"I think they were afraid of your reaction."

"Is that why you did not tell me about Lord Bronson? You were afraid of what I might say? When do you plan to leave me?" His voice was even and lacked emotion.

"I beg your pardon?"

"I received a message from Lord Bronson informing me that he had asked you to join him in London."

Stunned. She stood watching the play of emotions over his face. He was hurt, sad, and angry. She understood. She should have told him as soon as she had received the letter from Lord Bronson. Thomas might have been upset, but she was as well. She was furious that Lord Bronson had gone behind her back and informed Thomas before she had had a chance to tell him herself.

"Lord Bronson mentioned he had made you an offer to work for the Crown and asked for my permission."

"Did he, now?" She said as her frustration grew. "I was going to tell you. I planned to tell you today, but then I found out about your mother and Fitz. This is my decision, not yours. He had no right. Aside from the fact that what he proposes is secret, not many people know of the work they do."

"Lord Bronson believes that a wife needs her husband's permission in such matters. More importantly, he knew he could trust me. I was a military officer with an impeccable record, and Lord Bronson knows I am trustworthy. What troubles me is that he would ask you, without consulting me first. The work is dangerous."

"Why? Because I am a woman? Or because I am not intelligent enough for the task?" His only response was silence, which was vexing. "Did it ever occur to you that, like you, I would like to help others? I want to do something that makes a difference. I have no interest in becoming a nurse, but the work of a code breaker is challenging and interesting and I believe I could have a talent for it. I might fail, but I want to at least try."

He heaved a sigh. "I understand trying to do something others say is beyond your reach. You want more. I am not going to say that I wanted me and the children to be enough. That is selfish. Because of my...mother, I witnessed through her Ladies in Waiting the result of what it does to a woman. She was effective in so many lives." He reached out and cupped the side of her face with his hand. "But I am struggling with the decision to grant you permission. I have full confidence in your intelligence. It is the danger that worries me. You said you were going to tell me today. You have made your decision, then?"

"Perhaps I have. I would like to try. But I do not want your permission. I really dislike that word. It makes it sound as though I have not any sense and need you to make my decision for me. It is not your permission I seek. It is your understanding that this is something I need to do."

Chapter Twenty-Seven

The night of the ball, the air was crisp and clear as carriages rolled to a stop in the castle's courtyard. Footmen, in matching black-and-silver livery, opened carriage doors and escorted brightly dressed ladies and fashionably clothed gentlemen up the stairs to the entrance.

Elizabeth had joined Thomas to receive their guests. Cognizant of the eyepatch on his right eye, she stood on his left side, while he turned slightly toward the door so he could view his guests when they entered.

There had been a flurry of activity preparing for the evening's events, and more than a few mishaps along the way. But time waited for no man, and once they had set the date of the ball, they had had no other choice than to proceed whether they were prepared or not. There were still vast areas of the castle that remained under construction, and Elizabeth knew it would be years, not months, before it was all completed.

Since this was considered the country, and not London, guests had arrived early. She was grateful for the country custom of arriving on time and leaving before midnight. In London, guests arrived for an event fashionably late for an evening event and might stay until dawn.

There was a crush of guests in the ballroom. More than Elizabeth would have guessed possible in such a short period of time. Everyone wanted to meet the new bride. Except Elizabeth did not feel like a bride. She felt like an imposter.

She and Thomas had not consummated their vows. Therefore, in the eye of the law, they were not man and wife. She could leave at any time. Thomas would not challenge her if she requested an annulment. He was a gentleman, despite his claim that he was only a bastard. He had been adopted by a lord, which made him respectable in the eyes of the *ton*. But it was not what others thought of him that mattered, Elizabeth had come to realize. It was the puzzle of why he had been abandoned.

"I love your hair," Thomas said when the lull in the receiving line continued.

She felt the now-familiar flutter when he dipped his voice to speak to her in hushed tones. His voice was not that of a bored aristocrat or the patient doctor. His voice was intimate and meant only for her ears. "I will send compliments to Jocinda. She was most anxious for your response on my dress, as well."

"You may tell her my opinion is that you outshine the stars in the sky."

"Very poetic, my lord. But be careful, my lord. It is not considered proper behavior for a husband to shower his wife with romantic compliments after they are wed."

"I have my moments, and as for exhibiting the proper behavior of a gentlemen, I sadly admit that I have always failed miserably." He gave her a boyish grin that made her weak in the knees. What he said next stole her heart.

"But that is my opinion regardless of what you wear. So, I fear, I am a poor judge of the dresses you wear.

What about my appearance? My tailor and valet worked tirelessly but not quietly. More than once I overheard a lowered oath that a sailor would envy. According to them, I lack fashion sense and am incapable of standing still. They were pleased with the results, however. They should be. The bill for my clothes exceeded that of refurbishing the drawing room. And—dash it all! My cravat is too tight!" He slipped his fingers into the space between his neck and his cravat, trying to expand the gap.

"Here, allow me. You will ruin the effect. Your valet did an excellent job tying your cravat. It suits you. It is not too flamboyant, like some I have seen. A very conservative knot." She pulled his hand free and worked to loosen the knot. "You look exceedingly elegant in your new clothes. It is not enough that you are Lord Thomas Westerly. You must also look the part."

Thomas reached to tug on his cravat again, but she batted his hand away. "You prefer this version, then?" he inquired.

Her heart stilled for a moment as she met his gaze. It was an intimate question, one that went beyond what comprised appropriate attire for a person's station in life. "I prefer the man who was by my side when I gave birth to Jane." She resumed her task, then drew her hands to her waist. "There. That should feel better."

He stretched his neck to evaluate her theory and nodded. "Much better, thank you. You have a gentle touch. Sometimes I fear my valet is trying to strangle me." Thomas gazed toward her out of the corner of his eye. "It would probably be inappropriate, considering our arrangement, that you replace my valet."

She heard the question in his voice. It was not the

valet he wanted. It was her in his bed. She was attracted to him. How could she not? He was kind, patient, *gorgeous*, and loved Jane as though she were his own flesh and blood. What held her back?

Did she harbor lingering feelings for Derek?

The man had abandoned her.

Yet she had fancied herself passionately in love with him. He was everything the gentlemen of the *ton* were not. He had not been educated at Cambridge or boarding schools. He spoke inappropriately in front of ladies. But there were aspects of his character that fit the gentlemen of the *ton* to perfection. He gambled and drank to excess.

But he was still Jane's father. Because of Thomas's wondering about the identity of his own parents, she wondered if she should someday tell Jane about her biological father.

"You look troubled," Thomas said, in that deep voice he had that was meant only for her.

"Woolgathering, is all."

"Humm."

She smiled, knowing now the meaning of that particular response. He muttered *Humm* when he vehemently disagreed with her.

The footman struck his staff on the tile floor to announce a new visitor.

"Presenting the Earl of Willowdown."

Elizabeth felt Thomas tense beside her as he visibly straightened and took on his mask as a gentleman of the beau monde. Gone were both Thomas and Doctor Westerly. In that place stood Lord Thomas Westerly, adopted son of the old Earl of Willowdown, brother to the new earl and the lord and master of Glen Castle.

Thomas extended his hand to his brother. "We are

pleased that you could accept our invitation, my lord."

The earl was impeccably dressed in black. His breeches, gold embroidered waistcoat, and tails, were tailored to perfection. There was a diamond stud in his cravat, and a jewel-encrusted quizzing glass suspended from a gold chain. But his eyes were bloodshot, and his voice slurred when he addressed Thomas.

Although he knew his brother and Elizabeth had met previously, Thomas nevertheless introduced them with all the formality due a man of the earl's rank.

"It is my pleasure," the earl said, bowing slightly. But when his eyes rose to hers, Elizabeth forced a calm response. The resemblance between the earl's eyes and Thomas's *was* remarkable.

"You are most kind," Elizabeth said. "We are honored that you could join us. We hope your visits will become more frequent. We are family are we not? And I know our daughter, Jane, will be happy to see her uncle again, although it will be months," she said with a smile, "before she will do more than babble or gurgle a response."

The earl blinked in pleasure at Elizabeth's warm welcome and bowed again, with a quick glance toward Thomas. "It is you, Lady Westerly, who are kind. I will be happy to see your daughter again."

The earl bowed again and left to join the crush.

"That was odd," Thomas said. "My brother bowed more in the few minutes of our encounter than I have seen him do in my entire life. As lads, we joked that it was a ridiculous custom."

"He is lonely," Elizabeth said, watching him as he snagged a glass of champagne from a waiter.

Thomas followed Elizabeth's gaze and frowned.

"How could you discern that in our brief meeting with him? The two of you barely spoke more than a half dozen sentences." Thomas held out his arm, indicating that it was time to join their guests.

She rested her hand on his arm. "It was not what the earl said, but the way he looked at you when he said it. "I believe he misses his brother."

Chapter Twenty-Eight

Lively music drew the guests into lines as they danced the night away. Elizabeth had agreed on country dances, reserving the waltzes for another time. This set, the dinner set, was over.

The waltzes were gaining in favor and were considered one of the most romantic dances ever created. The popularity had something to do with the open disapproval of the older, more ancient of the *ton* who considered a dance where a man and woman touched scandalous. Elizabeth had no such reservations.

She had deferred the dance because she had not had the opportunity to ask Thomas if he had had the time to learn this newest craze sweeping Europe. The more she thought about the matter, the more farfetched it became. Thomas would consider it a waste to learn a silly dance when he could spend the time saving lives.

But as Lord Westerly, and master of Glen Castle, their guests might consider it odd if he declined to dance a waltz. Therefore, she had decided to take it out of the program entirely.

She scanned the dance floor. He was nowhere in sight, nor was he in the rooms she had designated for cards. She should not care… Still, where was he? The thought that he might be with another woman in a secluded alcove sent her heart racing. A servant perhaps? A woman from the village?

No, he was not that sort of man.

But really, what did she know about him? He *was* that sort and she had not given him a choice when she had made him sign the contract forbidding him from her bed. She was not naïve enough to believe he would welcome celibacy simply because the two of them could not have sex. He was handsome, virile, and she had seen how other women looked at him.

She snapped her fan open and fanned herself. This was nonsense and none of her business. They were not really husband and wife. Not really. They had never consummated their marriage. So, it should not matter who he slept with. But somehow it did, and that surprised her.

The evening was marching toward the dinner hour. Elizabeth winced at the dire thought. As a young girl in the schoolroom, she had looked forward to the time when she would have her come-out ball. She had dreamed of the dresses she would wear her first Season and how her maid would arrange her hair. Enamored with the opulence and romance of London's Marriage Mart, with the balls, garden parties, soirees, and fashionable clothes, she had not recognized its underlying intent.

All the glitter of the Season hid the sordid truth that women were on display. They were ranked according to their wealth and position, their beauty, poise, and their slender figures. Men would go to any length to possess the woman who had caught their eye. They would shower her with gifts, and flattery. They would talk of love, but love was never on their minds. Possession was the goal, and once wed, the woman would become their property.

Love matches were possible but rare. And that was

what held the attraction. It was the golden ring everyone wished would be theirs. The chance that their match would be different from the rest. Their marriage would be the exception. Husbands and wives would be faithful to their vows and love, true love, would last a lifetime.

She stood drinking her lemonade in a secluded corner of the ballroom as the dancers continued to form lines, then skip toward each other, only to twirl around each other before resuming their positions opposite their partners. This was her fourth lemonade, to be exact. Or was it her fifth? She had lost count. She discovered that a new mother, newly released from her confinement, was granted a limitless supply of excuses to avoid dancing and conversation. All that was needed was to feign thirst or exhaustion.

The dinner set was announced. She should find Thomas, but as though conjured from her thoughts he joined her, holding out his arm. "I do not intend to dance the dinner set, but can I presume that you will be my partner for dinner? You are my wife."

"You presume correctly, my lord. I do not believe I saw you once on the dance floor. There will be a scandal in the morning when news spreads that you did not ask even one young lady to dance."

"I loathe dancing. All that jumping about in uncomfortable clothes, when a good ride on a horse across the meadow would accomplish the same goal."

"It is not about exercise, my lord."

"Then what would be the point?"

His confirmation of what she had thought was confirmed. Usually, people who hated dancing simply could not dance and that made them self-conscious. "The point, my lord, is that dancing for the young and single is a form of romance, and a duty for those of our age."

"You make us sound like we have one foot in the grave. I for one, plan to live a long life, and I would ask you to do the same. Besides, I never saw the point of dancing."

"Dancing is an excuse for a man and woman to touch, flirt, and exchange innuendos that might lead to a chance embrace or clandestine kiss."

He raised his eyebrow. "A stolen kiss. Now you have my attention." He looked over his shoulder toward the orchestra. "Perhaps I could ask them to play one more tune before dinner, although my skills on the dance floor are limited, at best. I have two left feet and women would decline my invitation to dance on that reputation alone, if they knew."

She took in his broad shoulders, his boyish grin—and the black patch over his eye, which lent him an air of rakish charm. No woman still able to draw breath would deny the chance of waltzing in Thomas's arms.

"I would challenge you, my lord, on your last declaration. A woman would be a fool to turn you down. I could teach you," she said, lowering her voice.

His gaze traveled toward the dancers who had begun the set and would gather to proceed into dinner after the set was finished. He knew it was a lengthy set of music, having discussed it with the musicians earlier. "That would depend on the dance. The ones I have seen tonight look amusing, and I admit people seem genially fond of them. They hold no appeal for me. As I mentioned, if I wanted a robust exercise, there are other choices that come to mind."

"My lord, it is not about the dance itself. It is about the chance to gaze into your partner's eyes, laugh, converse, touch."

He crossed his arms over his chest and frowned. "But a simple conversation would accomplish that goal, would it not?"

Was he deliberately being so obtuse?

His boyish grin evolved into a smoldering smile. "I thought you would never get to it. Now, the waltz does hold appeal. And I would be a fool not to take you up on your offer. It is most men's dream to have an experienced woman instructing him on the best way to hold her in his arms."

She batted his arm gently. "You have been teasing me, have you not?"

He leaned forward. "Guilty as charged, my lady. I admit that I do know a country dance or two, but as I said, it is the waltz that draws my interest. Recently, my aunt hosted a ball last spring where it was performed. I declined to dance, but I can agree to its appeal. The chance to hold a woman of your choice in your arms, in full view of onlookers, was erotic."

"Erotic?"

"A fine word."

"A sexually charged word."

He winked. "As it was meant to be."

Her face warmed. He was flirting with her. "Dinner will be served after this set, and we would have an all-out rebellion if we strayed from the schedule. But where were you?" She bit down on the corner of her lip, but it was too late. She had spoken her thoughts aloud. They were man and wife in name only. She had no right to ask him where he had been—or, more important to the turmoil in her thoughts, with whom.

"I had more important business awaiting me. I was

in the nursery playing with Jane and Jonathan, as you were earlier, so Matilda informed me. It seems we both prefer our children over large crowds, regardless of how congenial or amusing."

"You were visiting Jane and Jonathan?" He nodded, but his attention was diverted when a footman begged a word. While Thomas and the footman conversed, her thoughts sped back to her own childhood. Her father had not been prone to affection. As a child she had believed that if she were good, he would change toward her. He never had, of course.

He rejoined her, a frown creasing his forehead. "What troubles you?"

She waved away his concern as she rested her hand on his outstretched arm. "A little tired is all. You visited Jane and Jonathan?" She repeated, her heart in turmoil. How could a man care for a child who was not his? It turned upside down every reality she had ever experienced. "I am a new mother and can be excused my lapse in judgment to prefer our children over our guests. You are Lord Westerly and demonstrating outward affection to your family and that is not proper *ton* behavior."

He placed his hand over hers. "Was that a rebuke, my lady?"

A strange warm tingling coursed through her when he called her *my lady*. It was her title, and it was used to address her dozens of times a day. But his use of it sounded more intimate. "No, of course not. I am pleased that you enjoy spending time with the children."

He gave a slight nod. "And it is a good thing then, as well, that we established that I do not fit what is considered proper behavior. If you are willing, would you care to teach me to dance the waltz?"

"Now?"

"But where? We cannot go outside on the terrace. It is cold, and a windstorm is brewing."

He offered her his arm. "I have a wonderful location in mind."

Chapter Twenty-Nine

The setting Thomas had chosen was like a delightful dream. During the daytime hours it was the playroom next to the children's apartments. The room was spacious and filled with toys to amuse a young child, from a wooden hobby horse, assorted games, and painted miniature boats to a child-size table and chairs. There was a rocking chair and a settee large enough for an adult to read while children cuddled next to them.

But Thomas had had it transformed to enchant all the senses. The toys were tucked neatly to the side, allowing space for a Christmas Tree, decorated with handprinted glass ornaments and bright red bows. A fire in the hearth cast a rosy glow and warmed the room. Candles occupied every imaginable space, and savory and sweet delicacies were displayed on a round table in the corner.

Overjoyed with Thomas' surprise Elizabeth impulsively kissed him on the check. "Oh, Thomas. You have transformed the playroom into a winter wonderland. It is beyond my wildest imagination. This is a wonderful place indeed."

He trailed his thumb over the side of her face. "You are pleased," he bent to kiss her on her forehead and lingered to whisper. "I had hoped you would be. I wish to make this night special for you. I know we do not have music…"

The passion reflected in his eyes flooded her senses and his nearness made it difficult to breathe. Her body hummed in anticipation of his touch, his embrace. "But we do have music," she said over the thundering beat of her heart. She searched the room, remembering a gift she had received from one of the Ladies in Waiting. "Ah, there it is." On unsteady legs, she crossed the room and reached for a music box made from inlaid mahogany and maple on a shelf and lifted the lid and cranked the handle. In a short while, the rich, romantic melody of Beethoven's creation saturated the room in beauty and light.

The waltz was considered quite scandalous, and until recently considered forbidden. She had laughed at such a notion and could not understand the reasoning. She had had her share of partners in the waltz and never understood why it was considered sinful…until now. She felt nervous as gazed into Thomas' eyes.

Elizabeth placed one hand on his shoulder and the other in his outstretched hand. When he put his hand on her waist, she gasped at his touch. His large hand pressed against the small of her back and pulled her gently toward him. She could feel the strength of his thighs through the fabric of her dress, and bit down on her lip to suppress another gasp. His heat radiated through her, each wave pulsating with anticipation.

He looked at her with such intensity that it stole her breath. "How should we begin," he said, his voice a deep fathom of want and desire.

Her breath came in short pants as she willed it under control. "The…the whole point is to feel as though you and your partner are one person. Feel the melody lift you to another place where only you and your partner exist."

"I would have you closer," he said.

She wanted that as well. "The rules say that we are close to each other when we dance but we cannot touch."

He winked. "A rule we already broke." His hand dipped lower until it rested on the curve of her hips. Then traveled lower.

"Thomas…" It is the belief that if we are close but not quite touching, it will heighten the couple's desire for one another."

"I must disagree," he said, as he lowered his head to trail kisses along her neck. "My body burns for you."

"Oh. Oh my." She closed her eyes as she tilted her head to accept his kisses. Her breast strained against the fabric and ached to be touched. "We should…"

"Remove our clothes?" He said, lifting his eyebrow.

"Dance," she said suppressing a smile. Every fiber of her being wanted him. They must slow down. If she lay with him there was no turning back. They would have consummated their marriage vows. The world believed they already had, and in its eyes, Jane was the proof of that union. But she and Thomas would know that theirs was no longer a marriage of convenience. But it was more than that. Meant more. She had made other vows.

She had vowed that she would never give her heart to another man. It shattered too easily. She pushed him a fraction of space away and cleared her throat. She needed time. "Please follow my steps in time to the music. Left-right-left, left-right-left."

He kissed her on the tip of her nose. "Your wish is my desire, milady."

The shock of Thomas respecting her wishes and not pressing his ardor caused her to lose her concentration. She stumbled, only to have Thomas hold her less she fall.

He held her closer than propriety warranted and had felt his arousal, yet he accepted her decision without argument. She had never met his like. The thick layer of defenses she had built thinned, allowing space for hope and possibilities.

Thomas followed her lead as they swept around the room, their steps matching the tempo of the tune, and the beat of her heart. Outside the windows stars peppered the night sky, blinking in and out as clouds drifted over them, occasionally hiding them from view. With each turn about the room, Thomas' proficiency grew. He twirled her in his arms, and laughing, lifted her off her feet.

She knew he lusted for her. She felt the same way. Thomas was handsome, devoted to Jonathan and Jane, and a kind man with a generous heart. But it was more than that. She felt safe with him. Safe in a way she had never felt before with a man. Even with her fiancé she had not felt this attracted. Her fiancé had been considered a suitable husband. On paper her fiancé had been the ideal candidate that all marriage-minded mamas wanted for their marriageable daughters and a man all single women sought to win.

Thomas was every bit as suitable as her fiancé had been. Only Thomas had that intangible quality that drew her like no other. He did not simply say that he cared about people. His actions proved his words. He patiently looked over his patients giving them his time, like he had an endless supply. When he asked about her day it was the same. The difference was that she felt as though the world stopped and it was just the two of them. He allowed nothing to interrupt them. She knew he was conflicted about her accepting the position in London and was confident he would change his mind.

But when he smiled at her…

Ah, that smile. It was as though it was reserved only for her. Her knees would weaken when he smiled, and her body would ache with desire for him. Jane Autin's novels had hinted at such things but for Elizabeth they had been the stuff of fiction. She had never dreamed of desiring a man as she desired Thomas. He was everything.

How could she not hunger for him?

Several times she broke away to rewind the music box, believing he would tire of dancing, only to have him sweep her in his arms and into the waltz. But on the third time she returned to his arms, he drew her closer, his hard body pressed against the length of hers. She gazed into his eyes and was lost in their depths as an understanding of what he meant to her crystalized.

She could no longer deny it or make excuses. She was in love with this man, deeply, hopelessly, completely.

For some, love comes like a bolt of lightning from the sky. For others, it comes slowly in the small everyday blessings and challenges that life brings your way. Trust was built, stone by stone, and with Thomas she felt as though they could build a fortress not only themselves but for generations to come.

Her lips parted as though of their own free will as he leaned down and placed a featherlight kiss on her lips. For a moment doubt roared. She forced it back down. She would take a chance. She wanted to love and be loved. She leaned into the kiss, relishing the heat of his touch, the gentleness of the way he held her as though she was precious to him.

He deepened the kiss as his tongue explored her warmth. His hand cupped her breast and teased the hard nipple through the thin fabric of her gown. She moaned and lifted her arms to twine around his neck. This was not her first kiss, but she felt as though this was the first time she had been kissed by someone who loved and cherished her. A kiss that promised a lifetime.

He whispered against her lips. "The night was made for love. Stay with me."

Her body heated under his gaze. She had never felt so alive. When he looked at her, she felt the world slip away. "Our guests…"

Thomas drew back and grinned. "You are a new mother. The ladies will speculate that you prefer our children over our guests. A few might complain that you shun your duty, while the majority will secretly envy your choice. The men, on the other hand, will know the truth of the matter. They will know that I am madly in love with my wife and want her in my bed."

Her breath caught and it felt as though her heartbeat was louder than thunder. He had said he loved her. She gripped the lapels of his coat and rested her head against his chest, feeling his heartbeat in unison with hers. Elizabeht was tempted to stay. Oh, so very tempted.

"Our guests can wait," she said, finishing her sentence, and lifting her gaze. "We have time before dinner. Do you have any suggestions?"

"A few ideas come to mind," he grinned mischievously.

He kissed her full on the mouth then moved a breath away. "As always, your wish is my command, *my lady*." He drew her toward the settee and sat down, drawing her beside him. "I would prefer the bed. We would have more room to maneuver, but with so many guests about, I fear if we leave this room, we will be interrupted."

"Very good instincts, my lord. You used the word, 'maneuver'? My, my. What do you have in mind sir?" She brushed his hair off his forehead. She adored the rebel curl that always came loose.

He murmured against her ear, the warmth of his breath fanning the fires of her desire.

"To love you."

The intensity of her need for him took her breath away and she gasped. No one had ever looked at her as he did in this moment. His gaze was raw, primal, sensual. His silent gaze spoke of passion, desire, and a need that matched her own. But there was also a tenderness in his gaze that spoke of love. She warmed under his regard and the question she saw reflected. He would not force her. He would await her answer.

She kissed his eyelids, then the curve of his lips. "Yes, oh, yes, love me."

****

Outside the night sky darkened and the moon shone pewter gray behind a thin layer of fast-moving clouds. Wind twisted through the branches, howling, and shrieking as it sped through the trees in the forest surrounding Glen Castle.

There was a change in the air.

The noise beyond the windows of the children's playroom woke Elizabeth from a sound sleep. She had dozed off after making love with Thomas and lay enveloped in his arms on the settee. Elizabeth closed her eyes and rested her head on Thomas' chest, warmed from the glow of their lovemaking. A storm brewed but inside the castle, she felt safe and secure.

She yawned, snuggling against his warmth.

Then her eyes snapped open. "The dinner." She felt a moment of panic and raised her head toward the grandfather clock in the corner, but it was too dark to decern the time. "You should not have allowed me to sleep. What are our guests to think?"

"I care not what people think. Your opinion is all that matters." Thomas pulled a blanket over her shoulders, kissing her on the top of her head. "But fear not, dinner has not been announced. We have time to make the grand entrance. Stay with me."

She turned in his arms to gaze up at him. "I wish we could stay here. Our guests will expect our appearance. We are the reason for the fete, after all. And your mother went to so much trouble arranging this dinner for us. We cannot disappoint her."

He drew her closer. "I meant, not just for tonight, but for always. Your life is at Glen Castle and Merwood with me. Not in London. If you are concerned that you will grow restless and bored, there is much here that can occupy your mind. My mother plans to expand Glen Castle to make room for additional Ladies in Waiting. She also wishes to open an orphanage with the purpose of finding good homes for the foundlings. She will need help organizing and making the arrangements and will need help."

His words swept over her like a glacial wind. He had not understood her reason for going to London at all. The explanation that she could help his mother with her endeavors was just a ploy. Thomas intended to keep his wife under his control. He might even have convinced himself that he had arrived at a beneficial solution that Elizabeth would find satisfactory. He could not have been more wrong.

She felt smothered and offended by his lack of understanding. She pushed away from him, discarded the blanket he had draped over them and scotting to the far side of the settee. Suddenly cold, she robbed her arms and crossed them over her chest. "We have discussed this before. I desire the challenge of learning something new. Your mother does not need my help. There are many of her Ladies in Waiting who she can draw upon. She does not need me," she repeated.

"There was never a true discussion, only two opposing views. You asked from my understanding, and I told you I believed your endeavor too dangerous. Even so, I told you I would think about it, and I have. I also consulted Lord Bronson on the matter. He said the code breaking work was confined to London but could not convince me that it was without its risks."

Her frustration rising, she scrambled from the settee and stood. "Risk is part of life, even at Glen Castle. I could fall from my horse, or drown in the lake, or tumble down the stairs."

He stood, his eyebrows drawing together in a frown. "Elizabeth. Be reasonable. You have everything a woman could desire, and I have proven how much I care for you."

"Was that the reason we made love? You thought it would entice me to stay?"

He snatched his trousers from the floor and pulled them on. "You know me better than that."

"I do not know you at all, nor you me. You say that I have everything I desire. That statement is false. I do not want pretty things. I want a husband who listens and respects me. Not someone who thinks they know what is best for me. I am perfectly capable of knowing what it is that I want. And using sex to entice me to stay is abhorrent."

His mouth formed a thin line as he clenched his jaw. "You are the most vexing woman I have ever met. The only reason I wanted to have sex with you was because I desire you and God help me, I still do. Need I remind you that you were more than willing?"

She perched her hands on her hips, her frustration heating to anger. "You called me vexing. An interesting and very civilized word, is it not? Well, you sir, are hurtful. You bedded me well, and I felt loved and cherished, and until this moment it meant as much to you as it did to me. What a fool I was. You labeled what transpired between us as nothing more than sex. I should thank you for clarifying our relationship."

"Elizabeth, you misunderstand. I was angry and did not mean what I said."

She huffed out a laugh as she crossed to a mirror to fix her hair. "Neither one of us understands the other. The perfect *ton* marriage." She frowned as she examined her reflection in the mirror. Her face was drawn, and she looked near tears. She blinked before they could spill over her cheeks. She would not give him the satisfaction of seeing her cry.

She refocused on her appearance. Her dress was wrinkled, and her hair had come lose from the pins and tumbled in disarray around her shoulders. She would use the excuse to change her clothes and compose herself before she rejoined him in the dining room.

"I look a fright. I will have to change otherwise our guests will suspect that we have had *sex*." She said the last word with venom. "I will call for my maid to do what she can and then join you downstairs."

He gave her a bow and without a word, slammed the door behind him.

Chapter Thirty

Elizabeth threaded her arm through Thomas's as they strolled into the ballroom past the Christmas tree shimmering from the glow of burning candles placed in holders on the branches. The small flames reflected from the red apples, ribbons, and holly that decorated the tree, and the decorations and their beauty momentarily gave her jumbled thoughts a reprieve.

They walked together like two strangers toward the double doors that led to the adjacent dining room, which had been decorated like a magical forest out of Shakespeare's *A Midsummer Night's Dream*. But like Shakespeare's play, the enchanted night was not at all as it appeared. She had not spoken to Thomas since their argument other than to mention that it was time they joined their guests for dinner. He had responded that the winter storm might keep many from returning to their homes and he would notify the servants to prepare rooms for their guests.

Making love with Thomas earlier in the evening had been like a dream, only now, did she realize that her time with him was bittersweet. The closeness that had grown over the last months had dissolved with their argument and had driven a wedge between them. He refused to understand why it was important to her that she have more in her life than being a wife, mother, and hostess.

Thomas did important work as a doctor. His aunt—

no, she must get used to thinking of Lady Tinsworthy as his *mother*—rescued unwed mothers. Elizabeth wanted to help fight against injustice, but there were few paths open for a woman. Lord Bronson had offered her a position to train as a code breaker in London, and that seemed like a sound solution. Thomas only saw the possibility of danger, not how the work she would do would help her feel as though something she did had a larger purpose. He did not understand and never would.

She had thought making love with him once would be enough. She should have realized that she would only want him more. She had fooled herself into believing that all she felt for him was physical attraction. She had denied the truth that she had begun falling in love with him from the moment he helped her climb from the tree. She loved Thomas so much she thought her heart would break at the thought of leaving him.

Doubt crept over her. She should decline Lord Bronson's offer. She would be happy helping Thomas with his work and Lady Tinsworthy with hers.

But she knew that was a lie. For a time, she might be able to pretend happiness. It would not last. She would resent him for blocking her path. They would become two unhappy people, locked in an impossible situation. That was not the life she wanted for either of them.

Thomas paused at the entrance as his brother, the Earl of Willowdown, escorted Lady Tinsworthy into the dining room and over to her chair at the head of the table.

Thomas kissed the palm of Elizabeth's hand as he followed his brother into the dining room and over to a chair designated for her at the opposite end from Lady Tinsworthy and the earl. "I fear you are further away from me than I would have wished. We left important matters yet to discuss. Are you responsible for this mad seating arrangement?"

Elizabeth sucked in a breath, momentarily lightheaded. Had he read her thoughts? Did he feel the distance between them as acutely as she had? Did that mean that he would tell her that he understood her need to go to London, and would not stand in her way?

She stood on tiptoes and spoke so only he would hear. "I confess I am. At the time when I helped Lady Tinsworthy with the seating arrangements, I suggested that I would prefer to be seated near the dining room's double doors if Jane or Jonathan needed me."

"Your first concern is always for our children and their welfare. They could not wish for a better mother. I regret our disagreement," he said for only her to hear as he covered his hand over hers. "If only…"

Her eyes stung from unshed tears, as she whispered a thank-you. The man was in torment. He wanted to protect his family and felt that the only way he could was to keep a tight hold on them. She guessed it might stem from Thomas being abandoned as a child. He was afraid to let go of those he loved. But love was more about trust than holding on.

"And you are an exceptional father," she said, unwilling to revisit their conflict. It would bring more pain. It was enough to know that he had regretted their argument. She had as well. But did he want to apologize or press his position? But what more was there to say? He had made it clear that the only position he would accept was for her to turn down the opportunity in London. Lord Bronson had made it clear that he wanted her husband's permission. But Elizabeth had learned during her time with her fiancé that there were always alternatives that could be explored.

"Perhaps when the dinner is over," Thomas said, interrupting her thoughts, "and we have bid farewell to our guests, we can explore something a trifle larger than the settee in the children's playroom."

He wanted to make love again, and now she wanted that more than life itself. She did not want to leave him with harsh words as their last memory and that was his intention as well. Her voice trembled. "I would like that as well."

"I am suddenly not hungry," Thomas said, kissing the palm of her hand again. "Perhaps we will not be missed." He spoke with a smile on his lips, but it did not reach his eyes. He was as troubled as she was.

"A tempting proposition," she said, forcing a smile. "Alas, we do not have a choice. We must take our seats, my lord."

They would not divorce; Elizabeth thought as she was seated. Elizabeth knew Thomas would never consider it and neither would she. She and Thomas would live separate lives. They lusted for each other now, but distance would cool their passions as it had done for many couples before them. Could she survive on the moments they carved out for each other? Could he? But if she chose London over Merwood, what choice did she have?

Thomas bowed farewell to her and took his chair at the opposite end of the table, next to Lady Tinsworthy. Elizabeth nodded to the guests that had followed them into the dining room.

The storm outside continued to rage. In contrast to the wild weather, inside the dining room, a crisp linen tablecloth adorned the long table, with a display of winter greenery, pinecones, and branches of candles. The three sterling silver chandeliers had been restored to their original glory, polished, and rehung over the table only this morning. A double fireplace encompassed one wall, while new draperies in forest green velvet framed the bank of windows that faced the ocean, where thunder rattled the panes of glass.

Shivers raised the hair on Elizabeth's arms as she leaned back against her chair. Instead of the scene evoking an oasis of serenity and beauty, the dining room took on an atmosphere of foreboding. Guilt over leaving Thomas clouded her every thought. She buried the feeling of doom and gloom. Glen Castle was a fortress. They were perfectly safe inside its walls. Tonight, she would enjoy the little time she had left with Thomas, knowing she would face tomorrow without him.

As though challenging her assessment of the castle's strength, a flash of lightning sliced through the dark clouds as branches scraped against the windows. Guests took in a collective breath and turned toward the sound. Lady Tinsworthy clinked her glass with her spoon for attention and announced that all was well and that it was just the wind, and they were perfectly secure behind Glen Castle's thick walls.

Her declaration soothed them, as she must have known it would, and her guests resumed taking their seats and sharing the events of the day and the weather.

Although Mr. Fitzwilliam knew Thomas felt it was proper for him, as his natural father, to sit with them at dinner, Mr. Fitzwilliam had declined, saying that his elevated position was still too new. Instead, he stood near Lady Tinsworthy's chair as he had done for decades.

Dr. Wilkes and Mrs. Potter took their seats near

Thomas. They had accepted invitations to attend. Earlier in the day they had assured Thomas that a team of doctors and nurses were on staff at Merwood's hospital to care for the injured. Elizabeth felt an unexpected surge of pride at their announcement. She knew their dedication to their patients was a reflection on Thomas. Thomas had surrounded himself with people who felt the same as he did regarding the patients under their care.

Lady Tinsworthy's Ladies in Waiting filed in to take their places, laughing, and chatting with one another. They were a lively bunch, in various stages of their pregnancies, and dressed fashionably in jewel tones and the colors of Christmas.

Elizabeth was pleased to note that Miss Turnby, who had asked to hold Jane when Elizabeth had first returned to Glen Castle, looked particularly fetching in a high-waisted long-sleeved cobalt blue dress. She was talking amiably with Dr. Wilkes, who seemed quite taken with her. The earl had set his cane beside his chair and was in lively discourse with Miss Waverly, who was also one of Lady Tinsworthy's Ladies in Waiting.

Miss Turnby and Miss Waverly were obviously Ladies in Waiting, yet Dr. Wilkes and the earl treated them respectfully as though they were ladies of the highest rank. Glen Castle felt to Elizabeth like a world apart from the judgmental *ton* atmosphere that permeated London society. Her throat tightened. She would miss the world Thomas and Lady Tinsworthy had created.

When the guests were seated, footmen brought in silver trays filled with sweet and savory dishes and began serving while a footman poured champagne into crystal goblets.

Thomas rose to toast Glen Castle's first ball in over a decade. He included his brother in the toast, welcoming him formally.

"I wish to toast my brother, the Earl of Willowdown," Thomas said. "Although I have recently learned that we are mere cousins, instead of brothers, you will always be my brother and best friend. Please accept my humble and heartfelt apology. I regret the part I played that caused our separation and wish only for your forgiveness. You are very dear to me."

The earl appeared moved and swiped at his face as everyone clinked glasses and conversation resumed. Then, leaning heavily on the back of his chair, the earl rose and lifted his glass. "Thank you, brother. Let us toast that we will always remain an important part of each other's lives." He glanced over at his cane. "Thank you also for mending my broken leg. I wish that everyone had a brother for a doctor. It comes in handy when you are as foolhardy as I am. Please raise your glasses and toast my brother, his beautiful wife, and my niece and nephew."

Glasses clinked again as conversation and laughter hummed around the room. Elizabeth turned her attention to the guest on her right, one of the newly arrived Ladies in Waiting, a Miss Cudworth, a woman in her early twenties. This lady wore a gold brocade dress that nearly matched her silver-blonde hair that was pulled back into a tight bun at the nape of her neck.

"You are looking well," Elizabeth said to Miss Cudworth.

"You are exceedingly kind. I feel like a lump. My child is due to be born in springtime, and I confess I am hungry all the time. Was it the same with you when you were carrying Jane?"

"Yes, it was the same. But as I am nursing Jane, my appetite has only accelerated, yet I am not gaining weight. It is delightful. I can eat whatever I like. I highly recommend the experience of nursing your child, not only for the sweets you can eat but for the closeness you will form with your child."

Thomas stood and clinked his glass for everyone's attention, then raised his goblet as he turned toward the guests. "I wish to indulge your patience a while longer. To Lady Tinsworthy. I owe her an apology. I behaved badly when she poured out her heart to me and confessed that she was my natural mother and Mr. Fitzwilliam was my natural father. Thank you, Mother, for your kindness, generosity, and love. You and my natural father have created a welcoming home for so many at Glen Castle." He motioned for Mr. Fitzwilliam. "And to Mr. Fitzwilliam, my father. Thank you for your steadfast loyalty to my mother and my family. And now I would like to toast my wife, whom I…"

The room shuddered and the table shook as goblets turned over, spilling wine. Chandeliers swayed precariously and wax dripped from their candles to the table. Guests watched hypnotized, and someone whispered, "Earthquake!"

The dreaded word reverberated around the table.

Thomas met Elizabeth's gaze and motioned his head in the direction of the doors leading to the ballroom. "A slight tremor but we should move from the windows," he said raising his voice above the rumble of the wind rattling the windows. "I suggest we leave the dining room without delay. I will instruct the footmen to bring cook's desserts and a bottle of port into the ballroom."

Trusting his warning, Elizabeth and the guests stood, pushing back their chairs as they rose to leave. Disbelief warred within her as she suspected it had with everyone in the room. Earthquakes were common in England and more of a threat to densely populated areas with tightly packed but poorly built tenement houses. But one must never underestimate the destructive powers of nature.

Another tremor rumbled beneath the table and a branch of candles tipped over, igniting the decorations. A fast-acting footman reached over and stamped out the flames with a cloth, as a new fear took hold. Fire was the most feared of nature's weapons. It had the ability to destroy everything in its path.

A cracking sound over Thomas's head froze everyone in place. The chandelier closest to Thomas dropped a few feet and swayed back and forth like a pendulum.

Then, like a game of dominos, it and the two remaining chandeliers plummeted from the ceiling and crashed onto the table. The flames from the candles on the chandeliers ignited the winter greenery and the tablecloth.

Fire leapt to the drapes as flames attacked furniture and chased up the walls.

Screams mingled with the clatter of overturned plates, cutlery, crystal, and the roar of the flames as guests crowded toward the double doors that led to the ballroom.

Thomas raced toward Elizabeth. "Elizabeth! The children! Run!"

Chapter Thirty-One

Thomas said a silent prayer of thanks as he watched Elizabeth dash from the dining room into the ballroom and then disappear. He needed to find a way to slow down the fire and give people a chance to escape. He threw a chair at the window, shattering the glass. Freezing rain poured into the room. It would take time for it to soak through the drapes, but it was a start.

Screams layered over the sounds of overturned chairs and breaking glass and brought him back to the chaos that surrounded him. He and his brother needed to take charge.

So far, the exit had not been blocked. Fires were unpredictable, so that would change.

With a nod to his brother, knowing Harry would understand, Thomas made sure everyone made their way from the dining room in an orderly fashion while Harry kept a cool head and escorted Lady Tinsworthy and Fitz to safety. Thomas overheard Harry instruct Fitz to take Lady Tinsworthy outside.

Once inside the ballroom, servants produced glasses and a bottle of port wine to the guests as though the danger was over.

"No place inside the castle is safe until this fire is out," Thomas shouted to his brother over the din of cheers and clinking glasses.

"Quick thinking on smashing the window. I agree

that it is futile to try telling your guests this is not the time for celebration. The rain is sheets of ice outside, and it is as warm as toast in here."

"It is about to get warmer. I need to find Elizabeth and the children. Lead these people outside—at gunpoint, if necessary."

Someone accidentally knocked over the Christmas tree. It toppled to the ground and the flames from the candles on the tree ignited the branches. They burst into flames and panic ignited as swiftly as the fire in the dining room had moments before.

Harry whipped off his coat and started beating the branches, trying to smother the flames. "Would this be a good time to tell you that I hate Christmas?" Harry said, laughing and shaking his head.

"Bloody hell!" Thomas grabbed his brother's shoulder, turning him around. "At the moment I agree with you. Live candles on a tree? An invitation for disaster if ever there was one. Do not worry about the tree. I need you to bring order to this bedlam or all the people in here will burn alive. Everyone must exit the castle as my mother and father did. I will take care of Elizabeth and the children."

"Be safe," Harry shouted, tossing what remained of his coat aside.

Thomas was halfway up the stairs when he heard his brother shouting for people to gather around him. Harry used his cane and pounded on the keyboard of the pianoforte to draw everyone's attention. The sound the cane made against the keys was sharp and shrill and ear-piercing and accomplished his brother's goal. The sounds of bedlam quieted as people gathered around Harry and then followed him out the door like the Pied

Piper of Hamlin.

Thomas reached the landing on the second floor and raced down the wing to the children's apartments. He yanked open the door and searched for Elizabeth and the children.

In the far corner next to the window Matilda paced, wringing her hands, and whispering that it was the end of the world. "Useless" was his first thought, then sympathy took over. Not everyone managed a crisis well.

"My wife," he shouted. "Where is Elizabeth? The children?"

Her hand shook as she pointed to the adjacent room.

Heart pounding, he raced to where the woman had indicated.

Elizabeth knelt beside Jonathan, putting on his shoes, while Jane wailed like a banshee in her cradle. Elizabeth's voice was deceptively calm as she talked with Jonathan and told him that all would be well. Thomas's pride in her swelled. She understood that remaining calm was key for survival.

A wave of intense relief washed over her as he ran toward her, pulled her to her feet and into his embrace. "Thank God! You are alive," was all he could manage. Time was not on their side.

Thomas scooped Jonathan into his arms as Elizabeth bundled Jane in a blanket. "We will use the servant's back staircase," he said. "Follow me."

Thomas led his family and the night nurse down the stairs and through the kitchen. Luckily, the fire had not reached the servant's quarters. He headed outside in the direction of the stables, which were a distance from the castle. His brother had realized the advantage as well and the people in his care were clustered for warmth around a small fire there.

The irony of the fire struck him. A fire was both friend and foe. When controlled, it provided life-giving warmth. When unleashed, it could destroy everything in its path.

Thomas scanned the crowd. His mother and father stood apart from the crowd, gazing toward the castle. His brother was nowhere in sight. The moment they locked eyes on Thomas, they shouted for joy and moved toward him.

With Jonathan in his arms, and his hand in Elizabeth's, he hurried over to his mother and father. He handed Jonathan to his mother. "Where is my brother?"

"Harry went back inside the castle," she said in a trembling voice, trying to hold onto the squirming Jonathan, who protested that he wanted her to put him down.

"My brother's a good man," Thomas said. "That is where I'm headed as well."

Elizabeth grabbed his arm. Her face was stained with tears as she held Jane in her arms. "Do not go back into the castle. It is suicide. Stay with us." Jonathan had wiggled free of Lady Tinsworthy and stood beside Elizabeth, clutching the folds of her dress.

"My brother, Wilkes, and at least a dozen or more of our servants are battling the fire. They need all the help there is available. Father, please use all available carriages and wagons and escort my family and the guests to the Rose and Thorn in Merwood. Do not argue," he said as his father opened his mouth to protest. "It is not safe at Glen Castle until the fire is out."

"I am not leaving you," Elizabeth said, bouncing Jane in her arms. "I am staying at Glen Castle."

Thomas dunked a blanket in a horse trough. "It was not a suggestion. I need you safe at the Rose and Thorn."

"Thomas…"

"Never forget that I have loved you from the moment I first saw you." He kissed her on the mouth, then kissed Jane and Jonathan. Thomas draped the soaking blanket over his head and shoulders and raced toward Glen Castle.

Chapter Thirty-Two

It was after midnight when a caravan of carriages, curricles, one barouche, and half a dozen wagons from Glen Castle clattered over the cobblestone courtyard that led into the Rose and Thorn Posting Inn in Merwood. Elizabeth adjusted the sleeping Jane in her arms and pulled a blanket over Jonathan's shoulders. Lady Tinsworthy rode in a carriage at the head of the caravan and had suggested that her grandson ride with her to the village. She had tried to tempt the child with sweets.

Elizabeth had been ready to protest. She wanted both of her children with her but would leave the decision to Jonathan. To her relief, he had insisted that he stay with her so he could take care of his sister, and that ended the discussion. At three years old, Jonathan grew more like his father every day. The boy was loyal, protective, and loving. She could not bear the thought that something might happen to Thomas. A child needed his father and Elizabeth needed Thomas.

She blinked away at the moisture that blurred her vision and drew the carriage window curtain aside slightly, hoping the torchlights on the inn would not waken her sleeping children. Thomas had spoken highly of the Rose and Thorn and that the innkeeper, and his wife were good people.

Thomas always believed in the goodness of human nature. That was one of the many reasons she loved him.

A tear traveled down her cheek. She ignored it as she leaned closer to the window.

Thomas's words still rang in her ears. *Never forget that I have loved you from the moment I first saw you.*

Elizabeth could not shake the thought that he had meant his words as a goodbye. She bit down on the inside of her mouth to keep from crying. Had Thomas been injured in the fire? Was he alive? Dead?

As the caravan drew up in front of the inn, a horn blared, announcing their arrival. Footmen, dressed in orange-and-red livery, rushed from the inn to help the guests from Glen Castle disembark as grooms tended the horses.

The loud noise awakened Jane in Elizabeth's arms. Startled, Jane threw up her little hands and opened her eyes, puckering her lips.

Jonathan, who had been sleeping beside Elizabeth, yawned, reached over to his sister, and smiled. "Do not cry, Janey. We are here. Isn't that right, Mama?"

Elizabeth drew Jonathan closer to her side. That was the first time Jonathan had addressed her as his mother. From the moment Thomas had introduced Jonathan, she had considered Jonathan her son and loved him dearly. The little boy had been told that his mother had died, and Elizabeth would never insist that he call her mother. Love welled in her heart that Jonathan had chosen this moment to call her "Mama."

She kissed Jonathan on the top of his head, smoothing the curls away from his face. "Yes, dearest, you are correct. We have arrived at the inn. Watch how your sister looks at you with such love. She was about to cry, and you quieted her fears. You are an incredibly good big brother."

The carriage door opened, and a footman extended a hand to help Elizabeth and her children. Lady Tinsworthy had already left her carriage and was headed inside. The Ladies in Waiting and the women servants and their children were also disembarking from the caravan.

She held Jane in her arms and kept Jonathan close at her side. She was pleased that he had begun talking to Jane and her again, because on the ride from Glen Castle to the inn, he had been somber and distant. He was a smart lad, and regardless of how many people told him to the contrary, he knew his father and uncle were in grave danger.

When Elizabeth and her children entered the beamed entry hall, she was warmly greeted by Mrs. Crawly. Mrs. Crawly was the innkeeper's wife and a jolly, middle-aged woman, with rose-colored cheeks and smile lines that crinkled at the corners of her eyes.

Mrs. Crawly curtsied and settled her arms over her ample waist. "We were saddened to hear about the fire at Glen Castle. Fire is a dreadful thing. I have never seen its like, and I have seen more than my share of weather's temper. Why, just the other month, poor Mr. Bramble's barn burned clear to the ground and with his chickens trapped inside. My husband and men from the village have joined your husband and the earl."

"That is most generous of your husband and the villagers. Thank you." Elizabeth was grateful. She worried, however, that help might come too late. She had witnessed the speed with which the fire had sped through the dining room. Elizabeth knew that the castle could be rebuilt, and possessions replaced. But if anyone died... The familiar catch in her throat silenced any additional response she might have given Mrs. Crawly.

Mrs. Crawly scrunched her eyebrows together and patted Elizabeth's arm. "There. There. I should not have gone on and on about Mr. Bramble's barn. My husband says my mouth runs away at times. 'Twas not my intent to cause you to worry more than you already are. All will be well. You will see. What you need is a strong cup of tea and a good night's rest. We will make you all cozy and the like, until you are able to return. A servant has shown Lady Tinsworthy to her apartment, and I have prepared an apartment for you and your children. We will also send tea and a light dinner to your rooms."

"Thank you again. Could you also send paper and writing tools to my room? I have a letter to write."

****

The next morning, Elizabeth ventured into the Rose and Thorn's dining parlor. She had tended to Jane's and Jonathan's needs and had left them in Matilda's capable hands. She had asked Mrs. Crawly if she had any word regarding the fire at Glen Castle and had received a disappointing "no" in response. She had then given the woman her letter and blunt to post it, before venturing downstairs for a cup of tea and a quiet moment with her book.

She found a cozy alcove overlooking a stream and a waterwheel and settled down with her book. Usually, she enjoyed reading. It transported her to magical places. She was particularly enjoying rereading Austen novel, *Pride and Prejudice*, that she had purchased at Merwood's bookstore.

Pride and Prejudice was fast becoming her favorite of the Jane Austen novels, although she said that with each book of the authors that she read. Elizabeht was particularly taken with its hero, Mr. Darcy. Although she admitted that as delicious as he was, she kept comparing him to Thomas and found that she preferred her real-life hero rather than the fictional Mr. Darcy. Was that the way it was when you realized you were in love? No one else could compare.

She could not purge Thomas from her thoughts. Elizabeth thought of him even when she was lost in one of Austen's books. When she thought of him, she worried. The fire had prevented them from resuming their conversation. She doubted that, without the fire, they would have resolved their argument. They were both too stubborn. The fire had changed everything.

Elizabeth closed her book with a thud and thumped it down on the table. The moment she did so, she rolled her eyes. She had neglected to mark the page. But if she was being honest, she had reread that paragraph at least a half dozen times. Her mind could not hold a thought that did not include Thomas.

She thumbed through the pages to find where she had left off and noticed ink smudges on at least ten pages. They reminded her of the ones she had seen when she had read the book *Emma*. They were curious as the smudge resembled a blurred line and only occurred under the word 'invitation'.

Her fiancé had been developing a book cipher where certain words were underlined to form a coded message. If she had not received the letter from Lord Bronson with the invitation to join him in London to learn code breaking craft she might have dismissed the smudges as an error in printing. The man was persistent. Should she tell Thomas? Ask for his advice?

"Come join us," Lady Tinsworthy said as she hailed

Elizabeth from across the room. Lady Tinsworthy was enjoying a cup of tea with Miss Waverly and Miss Turnby.

Startled, Elizabeth dropped the book. She retrieved it and gathered her belongings as a servant drew up a chair and prepared another place setting beside Lady Tinsworthy.

"Have you heard from Thomas?" Lady Tinsworthy asked, when Elizabeth sat down.

"I was about to ask you the very same thing," Elizabeth said. "I asked Mrs. Crawly, but she had not heard a peep. Is anyone as annoyed as I am that we were not allowed to help extinguish the fire?"

Miss Waverly had taken a sip of tea but spit it out when she choked on a laugh. "We were not informed either. Oh, I do like you, Lady Elizabeth. You say the most scandalous things. Gentlemen would be outraged at the thought of fighting a fire beside a woman. The men believe we are fragile flowers, do they not?"

"I agree with you as well," Miss Turnby said. "We should have been allowed to stay and help. Before I found myself in a family way, I was the only child of the village blacksmith and often helped my father at the forge. I am not afraid of demanding work, and I respect the nature of fire."

"Ladies," Lady Tinsworthy said, "your willingness to help is commendable and appreciated. My son is typical of his gender and inclined at over protectiveness. If we want to help, we might have to wait a few more days."

Elizabeth sipped her tea. "Waiting has never been my strong suit." There were times when she had been so angry with Thomas. There were other times when she buried her feelings, thinking she should make the most of the time they had left together. She had pretended even to herself that it would be easy to say goodbye. Now she knew leaving was impossible. But after their argument, what if Thomas no longer wanted her to stay?

"You are worried about Thomas," Lady Tinsworthy said, reaching over to take Elizabeth's hand. "I worry for Fitz and all those who are battling the fire. Fire is a terrible, destructive beast. It devours everything in its path. People still talk about the Great Fire of London in 1666. A hundred thousand people were left homeless! Some say it may have been caused by a spark in Thomas Farriner's bakery. After the embers cooled, all of London helped the city rebuild, and that is what we will do at Glen Castle. In the meantime, we have a wedding to plan."

"Wedding?" Mrs. Crawly said, approaching the table with a fresh pot of tea. "Who is getting married?"

Lady Tinsworthy slipped off her glove and extended her left hand. "Why, me, of course. Mr. Fitzwilliam has been asking me to marry him for years and I finally said 'yes.' We wed on Christmas Day."

Chapter Thirty-Three

A couple of days later, dawn broke over the horizon in ribbons of amber, red, and gold. Storm clouds that had sent a threatening message the night before had settled overhead as though waiting and watching. Dressed in shirtsleeves and breeches, Thomas had long ago discarded his evening clothes to tend the fire.

The dining room and the ballroom were burned-out shells, but the fire had not spread to any of the other downstairs rooms nor the apartments in the upper wings. Fast action by guests and servants had prevented the fire from spreading beyond the two rooms. They had formed a water brigade and doused the flames. But smoke lingered, and ash clogged the air, a reminder of how close they had come to disaster.

Thomas withdrew from the window in the bedchamber where his brother lay with his leg propped up on a pillow, irritated that he had been ordered to remain in bed rather than continuing to help with quenching the fire and with the cleanup. Thomas considered it a good omen that his brother's spirits were so high but cautioned against overconfidence. His brother had fought the fire at his side until he had passed out from the pain in his broken leg and ribs and had been carried to his room.

Wilkes dozed in a chair, his clothes as severely damaged by smoke and water as Thomas's.

Fitz peered into the bedchamber and knocked softly on the opened door. "May I have a word, my lord?"

Thomas woke Wilkes and asked him to watch over his brother until he returned as he followed Fitz down the hallway toward the stairs.

Fitzwilliam was as stoic as a monk as he descended the stairs and strode in the direction of the dining room. The man looked as tired as Thomas felt. It had been long days and nights for everyone.

Thomas smelled the lingering effects of the fire. The flames had been doused, and the smoke had permeated the ballroom wing of the castle. He had ordered Elizabeth, and all the women in the castle, including the servants and the children, be sent to the Rose and Thorn Inn in Merwood while the men fought the fire.

News had spread that the castle was engulfed in flames, and Thomas was gratified by the dozens of people from the village who had rushed to help. It had made the difference and had prevented the fire from spreading.

Fitz entered the charred remains of the ballroom. The walls and ceiling were covered with soot. The drapes had been torn down and removed, exposing blackened leaded glass windowpanes. The window that Thomas had broken had been boarded over. The chandeliers were a tangled mass of charred metal and had been tossed in a corner. It had stood as it was for generations and in a matter of hours both the entire ballroom and the dining room had been reduced to ash.

Thankfully, no one had been injured, and the integrity of the castle had held. They could rebuild. It could have been far worse. People could have lost their lives.

"I thought you would like to view the damage, my lord. These rooms are quite uninhabitable."

Thomas chuckled. "You are the master of the understatement, Fitz—or would you allow me to call you 'Papa'?"

An uncharacteristic smile creased Fitz's stoic expression. "That would please me enormously, my lord."

"You must call me 'Son,' or 'Thomas.' None of this *my lord* nonsense. I am immensely proud you are my father. There is no longer a reason to hide."

"As you wish. Might I say how happy your mother and I are. Lady Elizabeth is a fine lady and I have never seen you so content." His father swayed on his feet, reaching out for the doorjamb for support.

Thomas wrapped an arm around his father's shoulders, surprised how thin and frail they were. The padding in his father's suit made him appear more robust and youthful than he was. But his father had been middle-aged even when Thomas had first come to live with the old earl and his son.

"I am taking you to your room to rest. I will see if I can scrounge up something for you to eat. Doctor's orders." He grinned.

"My lord…" Fitz began. "Thomas," he corrected. "I must protest. There is so much to do. The rooms need airing, furniture and rugs must be cleaned and dusted free of ash, and the floors washed." He stumbled and would have fallen if Thomas had not been holding onto him.

Thomas slowed his pace to accommodate his father and berated himself. He was a doctor and he had missed the signs of old age, weight loss, and fatigue.

Thomas rounded a corner. "Your days as my

mother's butler are over. Why didn't you and my mother ever wed?"

"Mimi and I wished to wed, but she feared discovery. The old earl's wife openly disapproved of unwed mothers seeking refuge at Glen Castle. Your mother did not want to give the duchess another reason to try and close her doors."

"That is in the past," Thomas said.

His father chuckled. "It is indeed. After the duchess died, I continued to ask your mother to marry me. I do believe I wore her down, because she finally agreed to my offer a few weeks ago. We are to wed on Christmas Day. At least, that was our wish. I fear our wedding will have to be postponed because of the fire."

"Out of the question. You and my mother have waited long enough. Your wedding will take place on Christmas Day." Thomas laughed outright, shaking his head. "You are full of surprises, and happy ones at that. I insist that you move into the same wing as my mother. I have a feeling she would welcome the arrangement."

"I believe she would. Shall I send word to Lady Elizabeth and our guests that they are welcome to return?"

Thomas shook his head. "Not yet. Christmas Day is still a few more days off. We can invite them back the day after tomorrow. I prefer we wait until then. The fire has been extinguished, but I worry about the lingering smell of smoke. They should all stay at the Rose and Thorn Inn a little longer. I will make sure the inn has all the extra help they need. And what I need is for my father to start taking care of himself. Do I have your promise, or should I enlist my mother's help to persuade you?"

"Mimi is a formidable woman. She would have me

dragged to my room by force. You should rest as well," his father said.

"I plan to do just that as soon as I am sure you are settled."

Thomas realized he wanted more for his father than restored health. He wanted the man to have more in his life than work. It occurred to Thomas that he wanted to get to know the man better. After all, he was his natural father.

Chapter Thirty-Four

The next day, Elizabeth removed her wet bonnet, traveling coat, and gloves and draped them over the banister in the entry of Glen Castle. It was colder than usual inside the castle, but the chill did not cool her ire. The moment she had received word that everyone in the castle was well or had only minor burns, her frustration with Thomas returned vigorously.

He had not included himself in the message he had sent. He had not told her whether he had been injured. He would not have thought to do so. Always a thought of others, never a thought for himself. People might think it endearing in the same way Jane Austen's character, Darcy, originally kept valuable information from Jane Bennet.

Elizabeth was not one of those people. She was Thomas's wife. He should tell her everything, even if it meant telling her that he had aches and pains like other mere mortals.

And how dare he keep her away so long? She blinked, facing the truth. It was clear to her that he was still angry with her. She had said horrible, inexcusable things to him the night they had made love. She had accused him of seducing her to convince her to stay.

A weight seemed to press on her heart. How could she have accused Thomas of such deceit? No wonder he did not want to see her.

Lady Tinsworthy had proclaimed that she was going regardless of her son's wishes. Elizabeth had wanted to accompany Lady Tinsworthy, Miss Waverly, Miss Turnby, and the other Ladies in Waiting to Glen Castle yesterday evening, but it had taken longer than she had anticipated to hire a wet nurse for Jane and to settle the children with Matilda.

She understood the danger the fire posed. Lady Tinsworthy had related the story of the Great Fire of London, reminding everyone of a fire's ruthless ability to kill and destroy. But there had been little news other than the message that the fire was out and that everyone was safe. She wanted more details. No, she wanted a second chance with Thomas.

After securing the children, she should have returned from the Rose and Thorn the night of the fire. Yes, she should have returned. She could have helped Thomas with the injured. She could have helped him direct the cleanup of the castle. She had vowed for better or worse when she had married Thomas at Merwood Hospital. She had been giving birth to Jane at the time and admitted that she remembered truly little of the ceremony, other than the words "I now pronounce you man and wife." But still she knew the words "for better or for worse" had been in there somewhere too.

She was not an insipid wife who only stood beside her husband when life was jolly and carefree. The strength of a marriage was built not in good times but in bad.

Thomas had ordered her and the children from the castle until the fire was contained and the lingering smell of smoke had dissipated, deeming it unhealthy until then. He also told her that when he felt it safe for her to return, he would send for her.

Send for her?

She had bristled at those last words. The man seriously vexed her like no other.

She pressed her lips into a thin line. No, she would not consider his overprotectiveness endearing. She was furious with him. Her eyes brimmed again. She was furious with herself.

"My lady," Mr. Fitzwilliam said, scurrying to meet her in the entry as he adjusted the neckcloth at his throat. There was a lightness in his step as though he had turned back the clock. He also looked as though he had dressed in haste. "My apologies, my lady, for my tardiness in greeting you. You were not expected. Thomas said…"

There was something different about Mr. Fitzwilliam. She could not place what it was, but instead of referring to her husband as "Dr. Westerly" or "Lord Westerly," he had referred to him as "Thomas." Mr. Fitzwilliam had taken to heart Thomas's toast when he had acknowledged the butler as his father. Elizabeth could not have been more pleased.

The dark circles under Mr. Fitzwilliam's eyes had faded and he seemed…happy. It was that he no longer had to hide his love for Lady Tinsworthy or that he was Thomas's natural father. Guilt and lies were a heavy burden to bear and once released were a miracle medicine.

"Thank you," she said. "I am painfully aware of Thomas's orders to insist that I remain at the Rose and Thorn. I am here to help. Lady Tinsworthy mentioned that you two will marry on Christmas Day. That is wonderful news! I am so happy for both of you, but I know there is much that needs to be done."

Fitzwilliam smiled like a schoolboy. "Thank you for your kind words. Mimi has agreed to be my wife, and yes, there is much to be done. Christmas is only two days away. We are grateful the fire did not spread. The concern now is for the smoke, which is the reason it feels colder than usual inside the castle. Thomas ordered that all the windows be opened to help air out all the rooms. No one was injured, thank the good Lord, but I am worried about Thomas. He does not sleep beyond one or two stolen hours here and there."

Her instincts had been correct. He took liberties with his health. "Where is Thomas?"

Elizabeth admitted to the lingering smell of ash and soot, but surely, that was of minimal concern. What concerned her was that Thomas was pushing himself too hard. He believed he alone could solve all the problems of the world.

"Thomas is in the west wing with his brother, my lady. But he has given strict orders that the earl is to have no visitors."

"Well, we will see about that, won't we?" She was positive she overheard Mr. Fitzwilliam chuckle as she marched up the staircase. Each step emphasized how close Glen Castle had come to destruction. The paintings on the walls adjacent to the stairs were smoke damaged and would need cleaning, and the carpets were coated with a thick layer of ash. She picked up her pace until she reached the west wing.

The closed double doors of the suite of rooms Mr. Fitzwilliam had described as those occupied by the earl appeared like the gates to a forbidden kingdom. She could not barge into a sick room and give Thomas a piece of her mind as she would have wished. That would be disrespectful in front of a patient. Mr. Fitzwilliam had said the earl was doing well, but that did not give her the right to rail at the earl's doctor. The earl was recovering from a broken leg and damaged ribs and did not need to hear her make a cake of herself insulting his brother.

She took a fortifying breath. She would knock, enter when acknowledged, and if the earl were well enough to be left alone, she would ask Thomas for a word in private.

Her plan solidified, she knocked softly. Not hearing a response, she pressed her ear to the door and heard snoring. Presumably, the earl was sleeping soundly, and she surmised that it was safe to enter.

To make sure she had not misread the snoring sound, she edged open the door slowly. The hinges on the heavy door creaked. Startled, she paused and waited for someone in the room to respond. When all was silent except for the snoring, she slid through the open space she had created.

The earl slept on his back on the four-poster bed, his mouth open and breathing loudly. Thomas slept on the window's bench seat, his head leaning against the panes of glass and his legs outstretched in front of him.

The image shot straight to her heart. The infuriating man looked exhausted.

He had discarded his ascot and evening jacket. His collar was open, his sleeves rolled up at the elbows. It was apparent that he had not changed his clothes since the fire, and yet he looked adorable. He was also snoring as loudly as a train thundering down the railroad tracks at break-neck speed. How a man could look exhausted, be covered in soot, and still appear so handsome to her that her heart felt as though it had stopped beating was baffling. But he did. Love really was blind…and deaf.

It occurred to her that he might be cold. She reached for a wool blanket that had been discarded on a chair and draped it over his lap. Elizabeth placed her hand over his heart in a manner that she had seen Thomas do hundreds of times at hospital. He had mentioned that the gesture had two purposes. It helped him connect with the patient in a way he hoped would let them know he cared. It also gave him the opportunity to assess the pace of their heartbeat.

Relieved that his patient's was steady and strong, she smoothed his hair back from his forehead and placed a light kiss on his lips. "I am sorry for the harsh words I said to you the other night. Please forgive me. You and our children are all that matters to me. I wrote to Lord Bronson and turned down his job offer. I love you."

She had not planned to make such a long confession. The words had tumbled out of their own accord. It was because Thomas was asleep and could not tell her that she knew her words had caused him too much pain to forgive.

Silence gripped the area around where Thomas slept. Had his snoring paused for a moment? Foolish thought. As swiftly as the thought had occurred, the snoring resumed more loudly than before.

She must leave before he awakened.

She backed out of the earl's room, reluctant to leave, but leave she must. Thomas needed his rest, and she needed time to gather her courage to say to him when he was awake what she had said to him while he slept. Would he give her the chance to apologize?

When she reached the room's entrance, she squeezed through the opening she had left between the door and the doorframe and shut the door behind her softly.

As it closed, Thomas opened his eyes. "There is nothing to forgive, my love. I was the one at fault. Not you. I love you too, and I am going to prove to you how much."

Chapter Thirty-Five

A brief time later, in the ballroom, Elizabeth tied a
cloth around her head and an apron over her muslin dress
to protect it from ash and soot. The servants had been
gap-jawed when they learned her intent to help them
scrub the ballroom floors.

She pressed her hand against her chest for what
seemed the hundredth time. How had she believed she
could ever leave him? Thomas and her life in the country
had become precious to her. She loved him and the quiet
days and nights they spent laughing with their children.

Their children.

When had she commenced thinking of Little Jane
and Jonathan as *theirs*? The reality had occurred, not as
a thunderbolt, but softly and slowly over days, weeks,
and months.

She swallowed down a lump in her throat as she
swept the charred pine needles, ash, chunks of broken
candles, and the burned Christmas decorations into a
pile. She would need to get down on her knees to scrub
the melted candle wax from the marble floors. Glen
Castle would survive. The Christmas decorations,
however, were beyond repair. The hours since Elizabeth
had confessed to the sleeping Thomas that she loved him
and did not want to leave him had brought her more
doubt than reassurances.

Lady Tinsworthy entered the ballroom wearing a

dark green dress, a red-and-gold shawl draped loosely around her shoulders. She looked so much like a Christmas tree ornament it lifted Elizabeth's spirits. Lady Tinsworthy also wore a smile similar to that of Mr. Fitzwilliam when Elizabeth had arrived this morning at Glen Castle.

It was common knowledge that Lady Tinsworthy and Mr. Fitzwilliam planned to marry in the castle's chapel on Christmas Day. Gossip around the castle was that the two shared the same bedchamber, which the servants credited for the spring in Mr. Fitzwilliam's step and for Lady Tinsworthy's blush. The news had brought a universal cheer of approval and a joyful reason to clean the castle to make it ready to celebrate a wedding.

"What are you about?" Lady Tinsworthy said. "You help where help is needed, but shouldn't you be on your way to London?"

Elizabeth scooped the pile of debris into a bucket and wiped her hands on her apron. "I cannot leave you the day before your wedding. The servants are in the dining room doing what they can to clean and scrub the walls of ash and soot, and as soon as I am finished in the ballroom, we will begin decorating."

"Don't you mean that you cannot leave my son? If you leave, you will break not only his heart but yours as well."

Elizabeth knew the words were true. She had thought the same thing. "Thomas and I had a terrible argument before the fire started. He might not be eager to forgive me. It would be better if I left."

"Poppycock," Lady Tinsworthy said. "In most arguments, both people involved share the blame. Harsh words can be forgiven when the heart speaks its truth."

"I pray you are right."

Lady Tinsworthy bent to retrieve a broken glass ornament, turning it over in her hand. "In matters of the heart, I usually am. There is no use trying to recreate what was lost. All the Christmas decorations were burned in the fire. We will rebuild."

Elizbeth laughed. "You are not speaking of the fire, are you?"

Lady Tinsworthy wiggled her eyebrows. "Of course not, my dear. And you really must call me Mimi. You are my daughter-in-law and, I daresay, a good friend."

"We will make new decorations," Elizabeth said, "and ask the servants to bring in greenery and holly to decorate the banisters."

"A brilliant idea." Lady Tinsworthy dropped the broken ornament into the bucket with the debris. "I used to believe that celebrating Christmas year-round was utter foolishness. But displaying Christmas decorations in the castle brings such joy, does it not?" Lady Tinsworthy grew pensive. "Thomas has a great capacity to forgive. He has forgiven me and Fitz for our weakness of giving him away when he was born. I blame myself for believing that Thomas had been placed in a good home. I should have been more vigilant."

"Like you said wisely a moment ago, harsh words are forgiven when the heart speaks it truth."

There was a clamor outside the ballroom's double doors as Thomas entered with the wolfhound Finnegan at his heels. Thomas removed his gloves and tucked them into his pocket. "You have not left," he said striding toward her.

Finnegan trotted over to Elizabeth for a head rub, sniffed the broken debris, then headed over toward

Mimi. She knelt to hug Finnegan around the neck, pretending to ignore the conversation between Elizabeth and Thomas.

"You are correct," Elizabeth said to Thomas. "I have not left." Elizabeth felt unusually nervous. She had not expected the sight of him would cause her so much unease. His voice had been as it ever was when he first greeted her. It held a tone that said he was pleased to see her.

"If you had left," he said, with a smile, "I would have had to chase you to London and beg your forgiveness. At first, I believed I was dreaming when I heard you enter the earl's room."

"You were awake and let me prattle on and on?"

"It was a very nice prattle," Thomas said. "Did you mean it when you said that you loved me?"

Elizabeth retrieved a dusting rag from her apron and swiped it across Thomas's arm. "Of course I did, you irritating man. Why did you feign sleep? I was pouring out my heart to you!"

He took her shoulders in his hands. "At first, I was not sure why you had come to Glen Castle when I expressly told you to stay at the Rose and Thorn until I sent for you and the children. Then I thought you must be angry with me for telling you that you could not come. You are an independent woman who does not like being told what to do. I would ask that you be patient with me as I love you for your independence, but it will take getting used to."

She laughed. "You are learning, and I have much to learn as well. You want to protect us out of love, and at times I do not understand that is the reason you hold on so tight. Together we will learn from each other. I *was* angry that you ordered me to stay away. I wanted to help. We are husband and wife, and we are there for each other, not only in good times, but in bad."

"You are no ordinary woman."

"You have told me this before and yet it continues to slip your mind."

"A terrible habit I know you will help me break."

"You still haven't told me why you kept silent and let me think you were asleep."

He tucked a curl behind her ear and smiled. "I feared you would tell me you did not love me, but the moment you touched your hand to my heart, I knew."

"Thomas, you are a most frustrating man. Please do not speak in riddles. What did you know?"

"That you loved me as much as I love you. I behaved like the worst sort. You deserve to follow your dream as my mother, and I have. I do understand why you want to take Lord Bronson's job offer. Hopefully, it will not take a fire to make me see reason the next time we disagree. I posted a letter to Dr. Merryweather, accepting his offer to make me his partner in his medical practice in London. Dr. Wilkes will assume more responsibilities at the Merwood Hospital, and I will continue there from time to time. But my life is where you and the children call home."

She gasped and held her hands to her throat. "You must not do this. Your gesture is unselfish, and I love you for it, but it is too much. The hospital is your life, and they need you. You must not do this for me."

"I have a new life." He took her hands in his. "You and the children are my life. You must not elevate me to sainthood just yet," he said with his characteristic boyish grin. "When I wrote to Dr. Merryweather, I had a condition. He and I must never turn anyone away, no matter their ability to pay. I am confident he will agree. It was a topic we discussed while I was in university. And regarding the Merwood Hospital, as I mentioned I have made arrangements with Dr. Wilkes. I will spend part of my time in London and part at Merwood Hospital. There is no longer a reason to give up your work with Lord Bronson."

She loved him more now than she ever had before. "I love you too, and I cannot imagine a world without you in it."

"I have a surprise. Look who has come to help us."

Elizabeth turned in his arms. Merwood road was crowded with people and wagons heading toward Glen Castle.

"What does this mean?"

"The good people of Merwood learned of my mother and father's wedding and have agreed to help decorate. I informed them of the possibility of a second wedding." He knelt and held up a ring. "What say you to renewing our vows on Christmas Day?"

He produced a ring from his vest. "Lady Elizabeth Montgomery, will you do me the honor of becoming my wife?"

A large pearl nestled in a cushion of diamonds and sapphires and rested on an ornate gold band. "The ring is magnificent," Elizabeth said. "Wherever did you get it?"

"My brother said it was part of our family's heirlooms and he offered it to me as a wedding gift. Harry welcomes you to choose as many pieces in the collection as you desire. My brother is a generous man."

"That is kind of him," Elixabeth said absently, twisting the gold ban on her finger as she glanced at the ring Thomas held. "We do not need a wedding, however. We are already married."

"That silly ceremony at the hospital can hardly be called a proper wedding," Mimi interrupted. "What a splendid idea, Thomas! I do not know why I did not think of it myself."

"Need I remind you, Mother, that Elizabeth hasn't said yes?"

"Oh, she will," Mimi said. "Won't you, my dear?"

Elizabeth laughed. She was doing a lot of that today. "Yes, Thomas, of course I will marry you. But only on one condition. I do not need a new ring. I quite love the gold band you gave me when I was giving birth to Jane. It brings me happy memories."

"Well," Mimi said, resting her hands on Elizabeth's and Thomas's shoulders, "we have another wedding to plan, and in only a little under a day's time."

Epilogue

Christmas morning, the wedding day, arrived. An overnight snowfall had dusted the grounds of Glen Castle like frosting as the sun shone on the newly fallen snow, creating prisms of rainbow-colored lights. An arbor of winter flowers, built large enough to frame two couples, stood inside the altar of the Glen Castle chapel. Entwined together on the lattice structure were cyclamen's fragrant, heart-shaped leaves and pale pink flowers, winter violets, and the sweet perfume of clusters of pink and rose viburnum.

Thomas waited beside his father at the altar for his bride. His brother had agreed to be the best man for both men. Friends from Merwood, from the hospital, and the Ladies in Waiting all lined the pews on either side of the nave. Matilda held the sleeping Jane in the first pew, while Jonathan and the wolfhound Finnegan stood at the entrance of the chapel waiting for their cue to precede the brides down the nave.

"We are lucky," Thomas said to his father.

"We are doubly blessed, my son. We have found the women of our hearts and, miracle of miracles, they love us as much as we love them."

The wedding march began and everyone in the chapel rose and turned, then smiled in unison. Jonathan, his head held high and smiling broadly, strode forward beside Finnegan. He was dressed fashionably in a wh8ite suit, and a white silk pillow was tied to Finnegan's back. On top of the pillow were tied sets of rings—one set for Lady Tinsworthy and Mr. Fitzwilliam, and the other for Elizabeth and Thomas.

Lady Tinsworthy, holding a bouquet of white poinsettias, began her measured stroll toward Mr. Fitzwilliam, and when she reached his side, she blushed a rosy pink.

Then Elizabeth appeared, dressed in white lace, and carrying a bouquet of Christmas roses. Thomas lost all focus for those around him. For him, she was the only one who existed. He had told his father he was a lucky man. Those words did not begin to express how he felt.

When she reached his side, he took her hand in his and kissed it. "You are lovely. You quite take my breath away. Did you notice the Christmas tree beside the altar? It is a present from me to you. It is the tree you admired when we took the children for a walk in the woods."

"You made sure there weren't any bird's nests in the tree?" Elizabeth said with a smile. "We don't want to displace a family."

"My love, I knew you would ask. I truly love the soft place you hold for every living thing. I climbed the tree to make sure it was free of birds and squirrels..." He laughed softly. "...and kittens, before I chopped it down."

Elizabeth drew closer to him, tilting her gaze toward his. "You have taught me the enduring strength of love when it is built on mutual trust. Thank you for saving me on the day I rescued the kitten."

"I did not save you, my love. As I remember, you climbed down the tree without my help."

She reached on her tiptoes and kissed him lightly

against his lips. "You saved me, Thomas. You saved my heart and my soul and reminded me that there are good people in this world. I love you with all my heart."

The Vicar Chesterfield cleared his throat as he brushed away a tear. "Let us begin. Dearly beloved, we have gathered here today in the sight of God to join these couples in holy matrimony…"

A word about the author...

Pam Binder is an award-winning, *New York Times* and *USA Today* Bestselling author. Pam loves Irish and Scottish myths and legends, and believes in happily ever after. She is a conference speaker and the President of the Pacific Northwest Writers Association.

Pam writes historical fiction, contemporary fiction, young adult fiction, and fantasy.

http://pambinder.com

Thank you for purchasing
this publication of The Wild Rose Press, Inc.

For questions or more information
contact us at
info@thewildrosepress.com.

The Wild Rose Press, Inc.

www.ingramcontent.com/pod-product-compliance
Ingram Content Group UK Ltd.
Pitfield, Milton Keynes, MK11 3LW, UK
UKHW020658151224
452011UK00009B/39